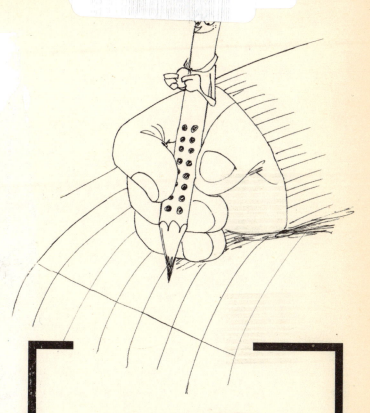

This book belongs to:

Penny
the Athlete

FABER-CASTELL
since 1761

Penny the Pencil has a proud heritage. She is made by the leading pencil manufacturer in the world, Faber-Castell. The Faber-Castell family have been making pencils for eight generations. It all started in a small workshop in Germany in 1761 and now the company employs 5,500 people worldwide. The company is run by Count Anton Wolfgang von Faber-Castell.

Faber-Castell is a company with great flair and vision. It is in the *Guinness Book of Records* for creating the world's tallest pencil at almost twenty metres high and has also made the most expensive pencil ever. The Grip 2001 pencil brings together these elements of design, quality and innovation. It has won many international awards. With its unique soft grip zone and comfortable triangular shape it has become a worldwide classic.

EILEEN O'HELY

Illustrated by Nicky Phelan

Penny the Athlete

MERCIER PRESS

WHAT YOU NEED TO READ

MERCIER PRESS
Cork
www.mercierpress.ie

Trade enquiries to Columba Mercier Distribution,
55a Spruce Avenue, Stillorgan Industrial Park,
Blackrock, County Dublin

ISBN: 978 1 85635 570 4

10 9 8 7 6 5 4 3 2 1

For Jasmina. With thanks to Reuben.

Mercier Press receives financial assistance from
the Arts Council/An Chomhairle Ealaíon

Printed and bound in the EU

Contents

Main Characters

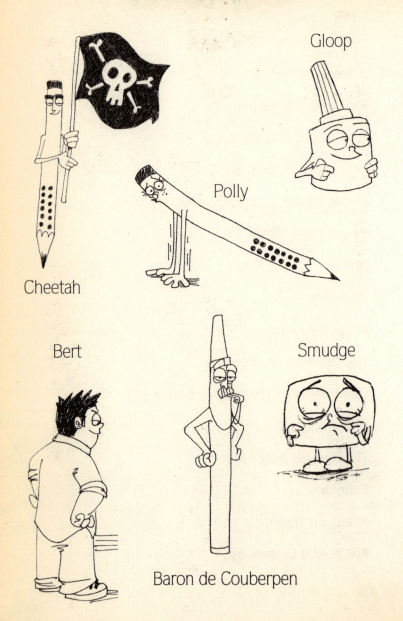

Gloop

Polly

Cheetah

Bert

Smudge

Baron de Couberpen

Penny

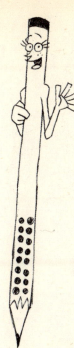

Sarah

Black Texta

Mack

Ralph

Mrs Payne

Chapter 1

A New Teacher

Brrrrrring!

The end of lunch bell rang to say it was time to go back to class.

Like children everywhere, the children in Mrs Sword's class were always disappointed when lunchtime was over. But the writing implements in their pencil cases were looking forward to the afternoon's classes.

A particularly large buzz of excitement went around the pencil case that belonged to a little red-haired boy called Ralph.

'Take your places please,' said Gloop, the kindly bottle of correction fluid who was in charge of Ralph's pencil case.

Ralph's coloured pencils lined up in two neat rows: one behind Penny, the grey lead pencil Ralph used for serious lessons like spelling and sums, and the other behind Mack, the mechanical pencil Ralph used for drawing.

Standing between Ralph and Penny was Smudge, Ralph's rubber. Although Ralph didn't make many mistakes these days, Smudge was always close by in case a quick rubbing out was needed.

The pencils' excitement grew as they heard the children approaching. Soon they could hear the familiar voices of Ralph and his best friend Sarah.

'I won fair and square,' said Ralph.

'You did not,' said Sarah.

'I even gave you a head start and I *still* won,' bragged Ralph as he sat down.

'It doesn't count as a head start if you only call "go" after you've run past me,' grumbled Sarah, dropping into the seat next to him.

'You're just upset because there's something I'm better at than you,' said Ralph, unzipping his pencil case.

'Hmph!' said Sarah, pulling out her own pencil, Polly.

To Polly's horror, Sarah also pulled out her sharpener. Sarah rammed Polly's foot into the sharpener and twisted her around angrily.

'Owowowowow!' yelped poor Polly as the sharpener filed her lead down to a fine point by scraping the off the outer layer of wood.

'Why is Sarah doing that to Polly?' cried Penny, peaking out of the open zip of Ralph's pencil case.

'Don't you get any ideas, buddy,' she warned

Ralph as he picked her up to write with.

But since Ralph was human, he couldn't hear a word Penny – or any other pencil for that matter – said.

Suddenly a piercing shriek echoed around the room. The children immediately stopped their chatter and looked towards the front of the classroom. Instead of Mrs Sword, their usual teacher, standing by the blackboard, there was an unfriendly-looking woman with a whistle around her neck. She was dressed in army fatigues, and her face was twisted into an unpleasant scowl.

'Good afternoon, recruits,' yelled the unfriendly-looking woman. 'I am your new Health teacher, Mrs Payne.'

'Health teacher?' Sarah whispered, sounding most disappointed. 'We were supposed to be doing Advanced Geometry …'

Mrs Payne picked up a piece of chalk and wrote four letters on the blackboard:

S-H-A-M.

'Can anybody tell me what this means?' shouted Mrs Payne, turning around and glaring at the class through her beady eyes.

Sarah, who had read every school book cover to cover, including the dictionary, put her hand up.

'A sham is …' she began.

'I beg your pardon?' shouted Mrs Payne.

'A sham is …' repeated Sarah.

'No, no, NO!' screeched Mrs Payne. 'And one hundred lines for your impertinence. What's your name, recruit?'

'S-S-Sarah,' said Sarah, blushing a very dark shade of red. As the smartest girl in school, she had never been told off in class before, much less given lines.

'Sarah *who*?' shouted Mrs Payne.

'Sarah Monaghan,' said Sarah, in a very quiet voice.

'Monaghan. Of course. I thought you'd be a handful,' shouted Mrs Payne, giving Sarah an extra-hard scowl. 'It's not sham, it's S-H-A-M, an acronym for Schools' Health Awareness Month.

'Has anyone heard of obesity? Rickets? Gout?'

The whole class looked at Sarah, but for once she had her hand down and her mouth firmly shut.

'These are the diseases that are threatening the very core of our nation!' boomed Mrs Payne. 'Primary causes are bad diet and lack of exercise. My mission, whether or not you choose to accept it, is to teach you good eating habits and get these sorry bodies of yours into shape.

'Pencils down! Stand up! Last one out in the playground has to do twenty push-ups!'

Mrs Payne blew her whistle to show she meant business. All the children leapt up and ran out of the classroom, leaving their pencils behind on the desks.

Chapter 2

Baron de Couberpen

When the classroom was empty, Penny, Mack, Gloop and Smudge hopped over to Sarah's desk to commiserate with Polly over her shared punishment with Sarah.

'I can't believe it, one hundred lines,' said Polly. 'And at the rate Sarah's going I won't have any lead left!'

'There, there,' soothed Penny. 'I'm sure that …'

An ear-splitting screech from the front of the classroom cut Penny off mid-sentence. All the writing implements turned to the front of the classroom where a khaki-coloured pen with a whistle around its neck was standing on the blackboard ledge.

'What do you zink you are doeeng?' demanded the pen.

'What's he saying?' asked Mack.

'Silence!' wailed the pen.

'And who would you be to tell us to be silent?' challenged Penny.

'I am Baron Pierre de Couberpen,' said the new pen in a decidedly strange accent. 'And I am goeeng to 'elp you achieve amazeeng zings'.

'What sort of accent is that?' Smudge whispered to Mack.

'I zink it's French,' whispered Mack, imitating the strange way the pen spoke.

'Is somebodee whispereeng?' said Baron de Couberpen.

'No, no, do go on, Baron de Couberpen,' said Gloop, giving Mack and Smudge a stern look.

'You!' exclaimed Baron de Couberpen. 'You are, wizout a doubt, ze fattest writeeng implement I 'ave seen in my entire life!'

Baron de Couberpen trotted from the blackboard ledge to Ralph's desk to get a better look at Gloop.

'You will be my greatest achievement,' continued Baron de Couberpen. 'By ze end of zis monz of SHAM, you will be ze slimmest, sleekest … what are you exactlee?'

'A bottle of *correction fluid*,' said Gloop, raising an eyebrow at Baron de Couberpen.

Baron de Couberpen went from khaki to a sickly shade of Kermit green.

'Correction flueed,' he said, swallowing. 'Of course you are. I am sorree. I didn't realise. No 'ard feeleengs, eh?'

'Just state your business 'ere,' said Gloop, earning a titter of amusement from Ralph's writing implements for mimicking Baron de Couberpen's accent.

'I 'ave a dream,' said Baron de Couberpen. 'A dream of ze most dareeng, most demandeeng, most delightful sporting spectacle of penceelkind. Ze Penceelympiad.'

'Pencilympiad?' said Penny. 'That's not a word I remember writing …'

'Of course it isn't,' said Baron de Couberpen, annoyed by the interruption. 'I just made it up!'

'What is this Pencilympiad?' asked Polly, hopping carefully on her newly-sharpened toe.

'A chance to win eternal sporteeng gloree,' said Baron de Couberpen.

The writing
implements' animosity
towards Baron
de Couberpen
disappeared as
they all imagined
themselves win-
ning eternal
sporting glory at
the Pencilympiad.

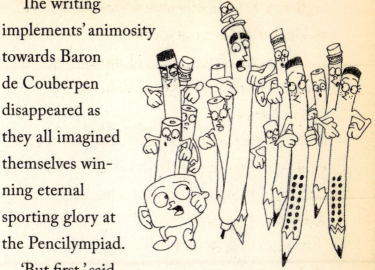

'But first,' said
Baron de Couberpen, holding up an arm, 'we
must discover 'oo is worthy to compete. I call
upon ze penceels of ze class to assemble into
four rows.'

Baron de Couberpen blew his whistle and
the pencils belonging to all the children in
Mrs Sword's class left their pencil cases and
lined up in four neat rows.

'On ze spot, and szog! Knees up!' yelled
Baron de Couberpen, bouncing on the spot
and blowing his whistle in time. 'Up, two, three,

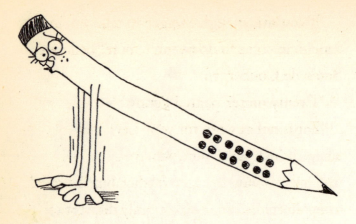

four, up, two, three, four. Zat includes you,
Fatso,' he said, looking at Gloop.

'What does *szog* mean?' asked Smudge.

'What's a knee?' asked Mack.

'I don't know,' said Penny. 'Just keep bouncing!'

Just when the writing implements didn't
think they could take any more, Baron de
Couberpen blew his whistle to stop.

'Everybodee on ze ground. On your front,'
ordered Baron de Couberpen, demonstrating what
to do next. 'And push-ups! Up, down, up, down …'

'I don't think I can take much more,' said
Polly. 'Even Sarah doesn't work me this hard in
a maths test.'

'If you 'ave enough energee to talk, you 'ave enough energee to do twentee more!' bellowed Baron de Couberpen.

'Twenty more?' panted Penny.

'Zat is not enough for you? Let's make it zirtee!' yelled Baron de Couberpen.

Penny wanted to argue further, but she didn't have the energy, and she certainly didn't want to risk Baron de Couberpen giving them even more push-ups.

With seven push-ups left, the sound of children's footsteps echoed in the corridor.

'March it out left, right, left, right,' boomed Mrs Payne's voice.

Baron de Couberpen blew on his whistle.

'Back to your desks, on ze double!'

The pencils all tried to do as they were told, but they were so exhausted from all the jogging and the push-ups that not all of them made it back to their desks before Mrs Payne marched into the classroom. She took one look at the mess of pencils scattered all over the floor

and blew long and hard on her whistle.

'LOOK at this MESS!' she squawked.

The children looked around the classroom with dismay.

'How did …?' began Ralph.

'NO ONE is going home until this room is ship-shape and you have written one hundred lines each!' bellowed Mrs Payne.

The tired children picked up their pencils and slumped into their seats. The hundred lines took them doubly-long, but they thought that was just due to the exhausting exercise class with Mrs Payne. Little did they realise that their pencils were just as tired as they were!

When Ralph finally put Penny back in the pencil case, all the other writing implements were gathered around the zip with worry.

'What happened out there?' asked Smudge.

'She gave them lines. Can you believe that? On top of all that drill training from Baron de Couberpen.'

'I don't think I can take a whole month of this,' wailed Amber, Ralph's tall orange pencil.

'A month?' said Jade, Ralph's little green pencil. 'At this rate I won't even make it through the week.'

'With Mrs Payne and Baron de Couberpen working together, I won't make it through to the end of tomorrow,' grumbled Penny, who worked a lot harder in class than all the coloured pencils put together.

'And what about poor Polly?' said Mack. 'Sarah already had one hundred lines to do.'

'She finished first, as usual,' said Penny. 'She's amazing.'

'I never thought I'd say this, but it's lucky Sarah gave Polly that extra sharpening,' said Jade who, as the smallest of Ralph's coloured pencils, had been sharpened the most.

'At this rate we'll all be whittled away to nothing before the Pencilympiad even begins,' said Penny, inspecting her toe.

'Hmph!' said Gloop, who'd been listening quietly up until that point.

'What's wrong with you?' asked Mack.

'I don't trust that Baron de Couberpen,' said Gloop.

'Because he called you a fatso?' asked Penny.

'No,' said Gloop stiffly. 'I don't like the way he's got everyone stirred up over some made-up competition when we should all be focusing on schoolwork. It was very irresponsible of him to leave you all scattered about like that when the children came back. Humans are supposed to think we're inanimate objects. He's not only pea-coloured, he's pea-brained!'

Penny and the others had never seen Gloop so worked up. They glanced at each other anxiously.

'Hey, relax,' said Mack. 'He's just acting like that because he's new in town. Give him a day or two and he'll settle down.'

'Yeah,' said Smudge. 'Remember how annoying Mack was when he first came to the pencil case?'

'Thanks, buddy,' said Mack, giving Smudge a look.

'Would you three knock it off?' said Penny, stifling a yawn. 'After all that exercise and writing, I'm exhausted. How about we get some sleep?'

'She's right,' sighed Gloop. 'We're going to need all our energy tomorrow.'

I sure am, thought Penny, *if I'm going to win the Pencilympiad!* And she went to sleep dreaming of herself standing on the podium, wearing a big gold medal for first place.

Chapter 3

A Not-So-Sweet Surprise

Mrs Payne managed to convince the principal
and Mrs Sword that it was healthier to exercise
early in the day, so from the morning bell
until recess she had the children running laps,
throwing balls, lifting weights, jumping rope,
and anything else she could think of to keep the
children out of breath.

'Out of breath means out of mischief, and I don't like mischief makers,' shouted Mrs Payne, patrolling the playground and making sure that nobody was slacking off.

By the time Health class was over, the children were completely exhausted and barely had enough energy to eat their lunch. Staying awake in afternoon classes was next to impossible, and even Sarah had to stifle the odd yawn.

When the end of school bell rang, Ralph and Sarah packed their bags to join their classmates in a slow walk to the classroom door.

'Ladies first,' said Ralph, politely letting Sarah go before him.

'Don't mind if I do,' said Bert, the mean boy who sat behind Ralph, almost knocking both Ralph and Sarah over.

'Bye-bye, Sugar. Night-night, Honey. I'll dream about you. Kissy-kissy,' mocked Bert, laughing cruelly as he left the classroom.

Sarah dropped her bag and stared after him, opened mouthed.

'Are you okay? Did he hurt you?' asked Ralph.

Sarah shook her head.

'He's a genius,' she breathed.

'Who? Bert?' said Ralph in disbelief.

'An absolute genius,' said Sarah, still staring after the bully.

'We are talking about the same Bert, aren't we?' said Ralph, feeling very puzzled.

'Didn't you hear what he said?' said Sarah, turning her attention back to Ralph. 'Sugar …? Honey …?'

Sarah stared at Ralph, but he only looked confused.

'I should make a cake!' said Sarah.

'You're making him a cake?' asked Ralph, totally bewildered.

'No, silly,' said Sarah. 'Sugar and honey give you energy. If I bring in a cake for morning tea, we'll get our energy back for our afternoon classes!'

'So the cake is for us and not for Bert?' said Ralph, brightening.

'Of course!' said Sarah. 'Wanna help me make it?'

'Sure!' said Ralph.

At recess the next day, Sarah and Ralph called their friends together to a quiet corner of the playground that was well out of sight (and

fist) of Bert. As Sarah pulled the lid off the cake
carrier, the delicious smell of freshly baked cake
wafted up everyone's nose, making their mouths
water.

Sarah counted the children and cut the cake
into the exact number of slices, then offered it
around.

'Mmm, chocolate cream sponge. My
favourite,' said Lucy, carefully choosing the
largest slice.

'This is scrumptious!' said Seán, wolfing
down his slice without even chewing.

'No wonder you won the county cake baking championship – this is the best cake ever!' said Ciara.

'It wasn't just me, Ralph helped,' said Sarah.

'Can you two make my birthday cake this year?' asked Malcolm.

Suddenly a shrill whistle blew. The children stopped munching and turned their chocolate-covered faces around to see Mrs Payne standing behind them, scowling harder than ever.

'WHAT IS THIS?' she bellowed.

'Issa jocrate ream spungake,' said Lucy, her mouth full of chocolate cream sponge cake.

'What is it doing in my playground?' demanded Mrs Payne.

Ralph stepped forward.

'It's my birthday today,' he lied, 'and my mum said I could take a cake to school to share.'

'Did she now?' shouted Mrs Payne. 'She can't be a very loving mother. Do you even know what's in sponge cake?' Mrs Payne continued in a scarily quiet voice.

The children looked at her, trembling.

'Eggs! The cholesterol killers,' boomed
Mrs Payne. 'Butter! Nothing but pure fat.
Chocolate! Second only to ice cream on the
scale of evil foods. And the worst ingredient
of all – sugar!'

Mrs Payne's beady eyes rested on Ralph.

'Ralph, isn't it?' yelled Mrs Payne with
distaste.

'Yes,' said Ralph in a very quiet voice.

'Your thoughtless, uncaring, nutritionally-
unaware mother has given me an idea,' said
Mrs Payne thoughtfully. 'I shall be sending you
all a note to take home to your parents. Make
sure you all wash the chocolate off your fingers
first. Your parents won't be able to read the
notes with your grubby little paw prints all over
them!'

In class that afternoon the writing
implements were having a wonderful time. The
children's extra energy rubbed off on the pencils
and they simply flew across the pages, writing

lines and lines and lines. Penny had been spending so much time concentrating on the Pencilympiad that she'd quite forgotten what it meant to do sums and write stories and circle the right answer in multiple choice tests.

Ralph was writing at such a pace that Penny was almost keeping up with Polly, and at this rate neither Sarah nor Ralph would have any homework to do, which meant Penny could spend even more time practising for the Pencilympiad.

Shortly before the bell rang, there was a knock at the classroom door. All the children looked up to see Mrs

Payne's face scowling at them through the little glass window.

Mrs Sword opened the door and stepped out into the corridor. She came back a few moments later with notices for the children to take home to their parents.

Ralph and Sarah looked at each other uneasily as Mrs Sword handed out the notices. They were very surprised by what they read.

In accordance with School's Health Awareness Month, Finbarr Community School has conducted a review of the products on sale at the tuckshop. Starting tomorrow there will be a new, healthy product selection, and parents are encouraged to allow their children to purchase items for lunch and/or morning tea. All products on sale, including drinks, comply with Standard 5.3.1.1 Subparagraph 2c of the National Health Food Act, which allows no preservatives, artificial colours or flavours. All the food has

been carefully selected with allergy sufferers
in mind, and will contain no nuts, gluten or
dairy.

'I guess there won't be any chocolate cream sponge on sale,' Ralph said to Sarah.

'I wonder what will actually be on sale,' said Sarah. 'Apart from no sweets or potato crisps, there'll also be no bread, cheese or milk drinks. Even the fruit juices had preservatives in them.'

The next day it all became clear. Armed with handfuls of pocket money, all the children descended on the tuck shop at recess. Their enthusiasm soon disappeared when they saw the poor assortment of food on offer.

'Turnip Twists! Yuck!'

'What on earth is a Lentil Lozenge?'

'Vegetable Allsorts, with one hundred per cent organic spinach, parsnip and sprout? Disgusting!'

'Maybe I'll just have a drink,' said Sarah when she and Ralph got to the front of the queue.

'Would you prefer fresh Grapefruit, Celery or Carrot juice? Wheatgrass is an extra ten cents,' said the lady behind the counter.

'Erm …' said Sarah, looking wistfully at the drinking taps in the playground. 'I'll have an apple instead.'

'Is that cake?' asked Ralph, leaning over the counter.

'Yes, it's carob cake,' said the tuckshop lady.

'What does it taste like?' asked Ralph.

'Well, it's the healthy version of chocolate,' said the tuckshop lady. She crossed her fingers behind her back as she told the white lie. While many women in her slimming club used carob to replace chocolate, it really didn't taste very nice at all.

'I'll have a slice,' said Ralph, giving the lady his money.

The slices of cake were all individually packaged in plastic. Sarah read the contents intently.

'Contains carob, rice flour, soy milk and natural sweeteners,' read Sarah. 'What's it like?'

Ralph took a huge bite and instantly spat it out.

'It doesn't taste anything like chocolate, that's for sure!' said Ralph, brushing the remaining cake crumbs off his tongue and giving the tuckshop lady an evil stare.

'Now, now,' boomed a loud voice. 'It doesn't do to be wasting food. Doesn't the birthday boy like cake any more?'

Mrs Payne towered over Ralph and Sarah, glaring down at them angrily.

'In my day, we didn't waste food. If we didn't
finish our breakfast, it appeared in front of us
again at lunchtime. And if we didn't finish it
then, we weren't allowed to have any dinner
until we'd eaten it all up!'

'It sounds like you had a terrible childhood,' muttered Ralph.

'Nonsense! It did me a world of good. I wouldn't be half the person I am today if I'd been molly-coddled as a child. Now eat that all up. Every last mouthful. There are starving children in the world who'd be grateful to eat the crumbs off your plate!'

And with that she strode off.

'Tell me their address and I'll post it to them,' said Ralph, waiting until Mrs Payne had turned the corner before burying what remained of his carob cake deep down in the rubbish bin.

Chapter 4

Penceelympic 'istoree

Early one morning the following week, Baron de Couberpen blew his whistle to assemble the writing implements for their own morning SHAM class after the children had left for their exercise class. The writing implements climbed out of their pencil cases to form neat rows at the front of the classroom.

'We will not be doeeng any exercise today,' announced Baron de Couberpen. 'Instead, I will tell you ze 'istoree of ze Penceelympics.'

'How can he tell us the history of something he just made up?' Polly whispered to Penny.

Baron de Couberpen blew sharply on his whistle.

'Ze Penceelympic Games 'ave a proud 'istoree. Zey combine ze most important features of being a penceel – neetair, sharpair, smoothair. While ze Penceelympic Games are open to everyone from all penceel cases, only ze best of you will qualify.

'If you are luckee enough to be selected, you will be competeeng not only for yourself, but as representatives of your penceel case. While zair are indiveedual champions, ze penceel case zat wins ze 'ighest number of points will be declared ze winnair.

'Zis is what we 'ave been traineeng for.'

The writing implements all shuffled nervously. Each of them wanted to be the one to have the chance to compete for their pencil case.

'Zose of you 'oo are not selected still 'ave an important part to play. Ze Penceelympic Games are not just about sporteeng achievment. Zey are about all ze penceels of ze class comeeng togethair in celebration.

'Ze Games will start with ze Opening Ceremonee. Each penceel case will be required to make a flag to represent ze owner of zat penceel case. You will entair ze stadium bareeng your flag, take ze athletes' oath, and ze Penceelympic Flame will be lit. Competition will begin ze followeeng morneeng.'

A buzz of excitement went around all the writing implements. None of them had ever been to a ceremony before, and they were all looking forward to it. Many of Sarah's coloured pencils were already planning the design for their flag.

'Ze Games zemselves will consist of five events, to make up ze Penceeltathlon. Ze events are: One 'undred Centimetair Spreent, 'igh

Szump, One Thousand Centimetair Row, Long Szump, and finallee Archeree. Ze events will be 'eld ovair five days, with one event per day, with gold, silvair and bronze medals for first, second and third place.

'At ze end of ze competition, ze points will be added up for each event, and ze winnair announced.

'To determine 'oo will be competing for zair penceel case, wee will 'ave ze qualification. Only ze fastest, 'ighest and strongest penceels will qualify.'

The pencils all started chattering excitedly, wondering which of them would get through the qualifying competition.

'Baron de Couberpen,' said a voice from the back of the pencil assembly. It was Gloop.

'Yes, Fatso,' said Baron de Couberpen, making Gloop wince.

'Is entry into the qualification round limited to one pencil per pencil case?' asked Gloop.

'A good question, my fat friend,' said Baron de Couberpen. 'Zair will be a minimum level acceptable for entree into ze competition. If multiple penceels from a single penceel case qualify, zen of course zey will both be able to compete.'

'That sounds very fair,' said Penny.

'Surprisingly so,' said Gloop.

'Zair will be a series of trials for qualification,' continued Baron de Couberpen. 'Ze top six penceels 'oo perform best at ze trials will qualify for ze Penceeltathlon at ze Penceelympic Games.'

'Oooh!' said all the gathered writing implements.

'Ze trials will take place starting next week. When ze athletes are decided, zay shall bee formallee 'onoured at ze Openeeng Ceremonee. One luckee athlete will take ze athletes' oath on behalf of all ze competitors.'

'Ahhh!' said the writing implements.

'Ze 'ighlight of ze Openeeng Ceremonee

will be ze lighteeng of ze Penceelympic Flame. Ze Penceelympic Flame will remain burneeng throughout ze Penceelympiad, and will onlee be extinguished by zee winnair – ze Penceelympic Champion!'

'Zair is one week left to prepare, so knees up everybodee. Up, two, three, four, up, two, three, four ...'

All the pencils joined in with even more enthusiasm than before.

When the sound of children's footsteps could be heard in the corridor outside, Baron de Couberpen blew sharply on his whistle.

'Quicklee. Back to your penceel cases. Anyone caught out of zair penceel case when ze children entair ze classroom will be instantlee disqualified!'

The pencils didn't need telling twice, and they were safely back exactly as the children had left them before the first child stepped into the room.

Inspired by Baron de Couberpen's speech about the opening ceremony, Ralph's writing implements put their training on hold for one evening and put their heads together to come up with a design for a flag.

'It has to be red, because red is Ralph's favourite colour,' said Penny.

'I agree,' said Scarlett, Ralph's red-coloured pencil.

'Red is a great colour!' said Mack, whose outer plastic casing was red.

'Red it is,' said Gloop. 'Now we need to think of a picture.'

'Why not just a plain red flag?' asked Mack.

'No,' said Gloop, shaking his head. 'We need something that represents Ralph, and all of us.'

'Something that represents Ralph …' said Smudge, thinking out loud.

'Well he's not very good at schoolwork,' said Penny.

'And art isn't one of his strengths,' said Mack.

'He likes to watch TV – we could draw a TV on it!' said Smudge.

'And he wants to be an actor,' said Penny. 'We could do one of those theatre masks.'

'Maybe something a little sportier?' suggested Gloop.

'How about,' said Mack, with a big smile on his face, 'a racing car! It's sleek like a pencil, it's sporty, it's red like Ralph's hair ...'

'It's brilliant!' said Penny.

'And it's got rubber tyres!' said Smudge, bouncing up and down.

'It sounds like we've found the perfect
solution,' said Gloop chuckling. 'Let's get to
work.'

Mack was the best drawer in the pencil
case, so he drew the outline of the car on the
flag. Ralph's coloured pencils coloured it in
while Smudge stood by ready to hop in if

anybody made a mistake. Even Gloop and Penny got to join in, Gloop painting a white number '8' on the door, and Penny colouring in the metal bits.

When the flag was finished, the writing implements stepped back to admire their work.

'We'd definitely win a gold medal for a flag-making contest,' said Gloop proudly.

Chapter 5

SHAM Physical Education Report Sheet

While Baron de Couberpen was inspiring the writing implements to exercise, his owner, Mrs Payne, was finding it harder and harder to get the children to do so. Instead of getting faster, they were running slower and slower, and the children were doing so badly in their other subjects that some of the teachers complained that the health food at the tuckshop was actually bad for their brains!

One evening after school, sitting in her lounge room, Mrs Payne was wondering what to do about the problem, when a thought occurred to her.

'What a champagne idea!' she exclaimed, her voice echoing around the room and making the windows rattle.

She uncapped Baron de Couberpen, turned him upside-down, and spent the rest of the evening drawing up a chart.

The next morning at school, Mrs Payne stood in front of Mrs Sword's class with a big rolled up piece of paper.

'I've been looking at your results,' she boomed, 'and they are shameful. Shameful! When I was your age I did one hundred push-ups and two hundred sit-ups before a two-mile walk to school, rain, hail or shine. YOU lot can't even manage ten push-ups, and your running is getting slower.'

The children looked down at their desks as Mrs Payne glared at them.

'What we need is some motivation!' Mrs Payne yelled, unravelling the chart she had been working on. There was a grid with every child's name running down the left-hand side, and the days of the week running across the top. Above the grid was the word SHAMPERS.

'What does shampers mean?' asked Seán.

'Did I hear an "Excuse me, Mrs Payne"?' Mrs Payne shouted at Seán.

'No,' said Seán quietly.

'No, who?' demanded Mrs Payne.

'No, Mrs Payne,' said Seán.

'One hundred lines for speaking out of turn!'

Ernie, Seán's little pencil, shook his head in despair.

'SHAMPERS,' continued Mrs Payne in her loud voice, 'stands for Schools Health Awareness Month Physical Education Report Sheet. Every day I'll be marking down how many push-ups you do. Every day I'll be marking down how many sit-ups you do. And, at the end of the week, if you haven't done enough, you will have detention until you finish all your exercises!'

The children all gasped.

'At the end of Schools Heath Awareness Month I will add up all the exercises you have done, and the person with the most will win a special prize.'

A buzz of excitement went around the class, and for once Mrs Payne let the children chatter amongst themselves.

The only child who was not excited about the competition was Sarah.

'Looks like we're in competition again,' said Ralph, nudging his best friend. 'And this time I'm gonna beat you fair and square.'

Sarah said nothing.

'And after I win this, who knows? I might enter the County Cake Baking Championship, since I did such a good job cooking that chocolate cream sponge ...'

'Oh, be quiet, Ralph,' snapped Sarah. 'Do you really think that a prize offered by Mrs Payne would be a prize worth winning? Look at the woman. She has no imagination. She didn't even use colours to draw the chart. It is all in that ugly khaki pen of hers. The prize is probably something like weeding her garden. She's looking for the strongest person who'll be the best at pulling out the weeds.'

'You know, you're as sour as that grapefruit juice you've been drinking,' said Ralph angrily,

turning his back on Sarah and talking to Seán
instead.

'Boys,' said Sarah, shaking her head.

Ralph didn't talk to Sarah for the whole of
the Health lesson. If Sarah even came close
to catching Ralph on the running course
around the playground, Ralph would speed
up so much that by the time Sarah caught
him again she didn't have enough breath left
to say anything.

At the end of the class, Mrs Payne added
up all the push-ups and sit-ups and laps of the

running course for each child. Ralph was clearly in the lead, followed by Seán and Bert. Sarah came halfway down the list, and wasn't even the best of the girls.

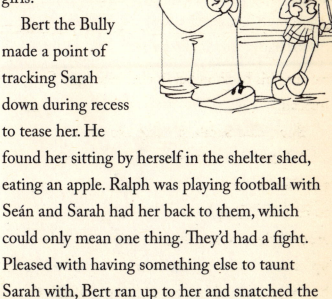

Bert the Bully made a point of tracking Sarah down during recess to tease her. He found her sitting by herself in the shelter shed, eating an apple. Ralph was playing football with Seán and Sarah had her back to them, which could only mean one thing. They'd had a fight. Pleased with having something else to taunt Sarah with, Bert ran up to her and snatched the apple out of her hand.

'I'm better than you are. I'm better than you are,' chanted Bert. 'You'd better watch out,

Monaghan, because I can run faster than you,'
he added nastily.

'I think *you'd* better watch out O'Leary,' said
Ralph, stepping between Bert and Sarah. Seán
was standing close by too, holding the football
tightly with both arms.

'Says who?' said Bert.

'Says me,' said Ralph. 'And by the look of
that chart I'm faster and stronger than you, so
you'd better watch out for *me!*'

Bert glared at Ralph a moment longer.

'How's the nose,
Bert? Healing
nicely?' asked
Sarah, from a
safe distance
behind
Ralph.

Bert
sneered at
them, then
walked off.

Ralph breathed a sigh of relief.

'Thanks for that,' said Sarah. 'And about before …'

'Forget about it,' said Ralph. 'I was being an idiot. Not as big an idiot as him, though!'

'I think it's really good you're winning,' said Sarah. 'And not just because you can scare Bert off …'

'Psst!'

A hiss behind them made Ralph, Sarah and Seán turn around.

Lucy was poking her head out from behind the shelter shed, looking devious.

'When I told my mum about the food on sale at the tuckshop, she made cupcakes. They're not as good as your chocolate cream sponge, but d'you wanna share?'

'Sure!' said Ralph, Sarah and Seán together, quickly squeezing in behind the shelter shed with Lucy so that Mrs Payne wouldn't see them and confiscate the cupcakes.

'These cupcakes are delicious,' said Seán.

'Much better than a stupid old apple,' said Sarah, licking the patty case.

'Want me and Seán to go get your apple back off Bert for you?' offered Ralph, much to Seán's dismay.

'It's okay,' said Sarah. 'Bert's touched it now. And if, as Mrs Payne says, you are what you eat, I don't want to eat bully germs and turn into a big bully.'

The children managed to eat all the cupcakes by the time the bell went. They checked each other's mouths for crumbs, hid the patty cases carefully in the bin so Mrs Payne wouldn't see them, and went to class.

Chapter 6

Pencilympic Trials

Things were beginning to hot up among
the writing implements in the trials for the
Pencilympic Games. Penny and Mack spent
every spare moment racing each other, with
Smudge cheering for Penny and Little Mack

offering Mack lots of good advice. Both of them were faster than the qualification time, and all the writing implements in Ralph's pencil case thought it would be great if they could have two entrants in the Pencilympic Games. Gloop was very impressed with the way all the pencils rallied around and supported each other, and began to think that maybe Baron de Couberpen wasn't such a bad old stick after all.

The night before the trials Penny hardly slept a wink.

'Would you stop all your tossing and turning?' complained Mack. 'I need all my strength for the big day tomorrow!'

'I can't help it,' said Penny. 'I'm too excited!'

'If I don't win, I know who to blame then,' said Mack, rolling over and screwing his eyes shut tight.

When morning finally came, Penny was the first out of bed.

'Stop all that bouncing around,' said Gloop. 'You need to save your energy for the trials.'

Penny barely managed a squeak in reply.

Ralph seemed to take an eternity packing his school bag and walking to school that morning.

'Why's he taking so long? Doesn't he know what day it is?' said Penny.

'Of course not,' said Gloop. 'Those humans haven't the faintest idea what their pencils get up to when they're not around.'

Even after Ralph gets to school, Penny still had to wait for the bell to ring and Mrs Payne to blow her whistle to summon the children to the playground.

'Stop hopping around like that,' said Mack. 'You're making me nervous.'

Finally the bell rang, shortly followed by Mrs Payne blowing on her whistle. As soon as the children had filed out of the classroom, the pencil cases on every desk burst open, the hopeful competitors gathering at the front of the classroom before Baron de Couberpen had even blown his whistle.

'My, my, we have some eager penceels for ze trials zis morneeng,' said Baron de Couberpen. 'Welcome everybodee to ze trials for ze Classroom 3B Penceelympiad.'

All the writing implements clapped.

'Zis morneeng, ze finest athletes from each child's penceel case will compete for ze shance to star in ze Penceelympic event, ze Penceeltathlon,' continued Baron de Couberpen. 'Ze trials will consist of three 'eats. Ze six penceels who have ze 'ighest combined score in all of zair 'eats will qualify for ze Penceeltathlon.'

Penny noticed several pencils shuffling nervously. Even Polly, the most confident pencil Penny knew, seemed quite anxious.

'Ze first event is ze 'undred centimetair sprint. Would ze competitors take zair marks at ze starting line.'

While Baron de Couberpen had been speaking, the sticks of chalk had been hard at work drawing lanes on the floor under the blackboard. The lanes were one hundred centimetres long, with 'START' written across one end and 'FINISH' written at the other.

Penny, Mack, Polly and all the other hopeful pencils made their way to the starting line, while the others gathered at the sides of the race course in their pencil case groups.

'On your marks. Get set. Go!' shouted Baron de Couberpen, blowing sharply on his whistle.

The competing pencils took off, sprinting along their lanes towards the finish line. In just a few hops, Penny, Mack, Polly, Seán the Chewer's little pencil Ernie, a red-and-white striped pencil and a yellow pencil with black spots were

ahead of all the other pencils. Penny and Mack
bounced along easily, their extra training putting
them ahead of the others in no time.

Suddenly, a green pencil with orange flowers
on it came up on Penny's right and overtook
her. Penny and Mack looked at each other, then
hopped faster. Penny pulled ahead of Mack, and
started gaining on the flowery pencil, but it was
too late. The orange flowery pencil had already

crossed the finish line, and was bowing to the applause of all the spectators, particularly those from Ciara's pencil case.

Penny finished second, followed by Mack, Polly, the yellow pencil with the black spots and the red-and-white striped pencil.

Baron de Couberpen made his way through the cheering pencils.

'Your name please, *Mademoiselle*,' he said to the winning pencil.

'Fleur,' said the pencil.

'Penceel case?' continued Baron de Couberpen.

'Ciara's,' said Fleur.

Baron de Couberpen took the names of the other pencils. Penny and Polly were surprised not to have recognised Stripes, the red-and-white striped pencil from Lucy's pencil case. And they were very surprised to learn that the yellow pencil with black spots came from Bert's pencil case, and was called Cheetah.

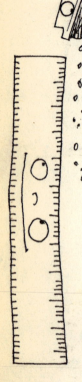

'Congratulations to
our six winnairs,' said
Baron de Couberpen. 'Of
course, zis is only ze first
of three trial events, so we
may indeed see a different six
Penceelympians at ze end of zis
morneeng's trial. Ze next 'eat is
'igh szump. Would ze competitors
take zair places again at ze starting
line.'

Penny, Mack, Polly, and the
other pencils lined up.

'Turn to your left!' said Baron de
Couberpen.

Penny and the other competitors
turned to their left. To their surprise they
saw a ruler standing on its end, and above
it, two blackboard dusters slapping their bellies
together and making a shower of chalk dust.

'As zis is a trial,' said Baron de Couberpen,
'you will 'ave only one szump. We will measure

74

your progress by ze hole you leave in ze chalk dust on the ruler. First competitair!'

The first pencil to have a go at the high jump was Ernie. He took a short run-up, then bounced so high Penny could hardly believe it. Ernie made a hole in the chalk dust that was much higher than he was tall.

The funny assortment of bitten and chewed pencils that lived in Seán the Chewer's pencil case bounced up and down with excitement.

The other pencils took their turns one after the other, the writing implements of their particular pencil case cheering loudly, whether the pencils did well or not.

Before long it was Mack's turn.

'Good luck,' said Penny, as Baron de

Couberpen gave Mack the signal, saying it was safe to jump.

Mack started his run-up and leapt. He sailed through the chalk, leaving a gaping hole six centimetres higher than the previous best pencil. Ralph's pencils went beserk, then looked on keenly as it was Penny's turn.

'Come on, Penny. You can do it!' said Polly, supportively.

Penny was extremely nervous, particularly with so many people watching her. She took a deep breath, then began her run-up. When she got to the ruler, she sprang into the air, making a hole a couple of centimetres below Mack's.

All of Ralph's pencils jumped up and down just as excitedly for Penny as they had for Mack, even though her jump hadn't been as high. When the official results were written up on the blackboard, Penny was in fourth place. But with three pencils to go, she wasn't guaranteed a place in the final – especially because the three pencils left were Polly, Cheetah and of course the winner of the sprint, Fleur.

Penny crossed her fingers, hoping that Polly would do a good jump and make the final.

Polly took her run-up, leapt up, and soared through the air, half a centimetre higher than Penny, putting Polly in fourth place. With only two more jumpers to go, Polly had definitely made the top six.

Sarah's pencils went wild.

Penny was also very happy for her friend, but a bit nervous of her place in the final.

Next it was Fleur's go.

Ciara's pencils all chanted 'Fle-ur! Fle-ur!' as Fleur took her run-up. Being such a fast runner, Fleur reached the ruler in no time and took off. The hole Fleur made in the chalk dust seemed to be much higher than Polly's jump, and all of Ciara's pencils started singing. However, there was a big 'Boo!' when the results were written on the blackboard. Fleur's jump measured two centimetres lower than Penny's.

That can't be right, Penny thought to herself. She looked around the classroom and noticed that while most of the writing implements seemed to be outraged at the scoring, there was one group who wasn't: Bert's. And when Penny turned to look at Cheetah, he was smirking.

Penny narrowed her eyes as Cheetah the Cheater took his run-up. He flew into the air and just scraped into sixth place, ahead of Fleur but behind Penny.

Bert's pencils ran out onto the field to congratulate Cheetah, who looked very smug indeed.

'Zat is ze end of ze 'igh szump,' announced Baron de Couberpen. 'Ze combined scores from 'eats one and two are: first place, Mack!'

All Ralph's writing implements cheered and clapped.

'Second place, Pennee!'

Penny was surprised to be in second place, but when she looked at the scores on the blackboard it all added up.

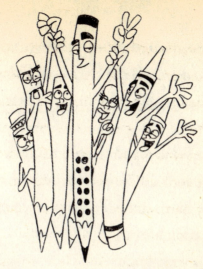

'Zird place, we 'ave a four-way tie between Fleur, Pollee, Stripes and Airnee. Zay are our top six.'

Cheetah stopped smiling and scowled at Baron de Couberpen. Then he whipped his head around and looked at the scores on the blackboard. He was in seventh place, just out of the top six, but he was quite a few points behind those in third place. If he was to make the final six, he'd have to do really well in the long jump.

As Penny watched, Cheetah had a quiet word with his pencil case mates, some of whom disappeared into the crowd as though they were on a mission. Penny decided to keep a close watch on Cheetah during the final heat.

'We 'ave one round to go, and anyzeeng could 'appen,' said Baron de Couberpen. 'Ze final is ze long szump. To make ze competition more exciteeng, would ze competitairs please stand in reverse points ordair.'

The competing pencils mingled around the start area, not sure what reverse points order was. Penny thought she saw one of Bert's other pencils pass something to Cheetah, but it was hard to tell in all the confusion. Before Penny could get close enough to Cheetah to see what it was, Baron de Couberpen had decided to marshal the pencils into the correct order himself.

"Oo is ze losair?' he asked.

The three pencils from Malcolm's pencil case put up their hands. They had tied for last in the hundred centimetre sprint, and one of them had jumped so low in the high jump that it seemed as though he had burrowed under the carpet to get to the other side.

'Losairs up zis end, winnairs up zat end,' said Baron de Couberpen.

With a little shuffling the pencils finally get in the right order – the ones with the lowest points at the front of the line, and Penny and Mack at the back. Penny was happy to be facing down the line, because it meant she could keep an eye on Cheetah.

Baron de Couberpen blew his whistle and the first of Malcolm's pencils ran towards the jump line. Her run-up wasn't very fast, and her jump was so short she didn't even reach the landing pad! Baron de Couberpen shook his head as he wrote down her score.

Malcolm's second pencil then took off. He was faster, but halfway down he tripped and tumbled head over toe through the air, also landing short of the pad. Malcolm's third pencil did no better, but put on a comic performance that drew laughs and claps from the spectators.

'Did you see that?' asked Polly, turning to Penny and momentarily blocking Penny's view of Cheetah.

'See what?' said Penny distractedly, moving so she could get a better view of Cheetah.

'What's wrong, Penny?' asked Polly, noticing Penny's strange behaviour.

'I don't trust Cheetah,' whispered Penny. 'I think he's up to something and we'd all better watch out.'

'Just because he's Bert's pencil, and has an unfortunate-sounding name doesn't mean we shouldn't trust him,' whispered Polly back.

'But just before,' said Penny urgently, 'he really looked like a cheater.'

'I think he looks more like a leopard …' said Polly.

'I'm not talking about his spots,' said Penny. 'I'm talking about the way he behaved when Baron de Couberpen announced the scores. He had this smirk on his face. And just now I'm fairly sure one of Bert's pencils passed him something.'

Penny quickly filled Polly in on her earlier observations. Mack, who was behind Penny in the starting line, listened in too.

'So you really think he sabotaged the score for Fleur's jump?' asked Mack.

'I think he's going to try something in this round too,' said Penny. 'And this time it won't just be the score. We'd better be careful.'

Penny looked up again, just as Baron de Couberpen blew the whistle for Cheetah's turn.

Cheetah started his run-up. When he got to the jump line he flung his arms and fingers wide and launched himself forwards, flying further than anyone else and landing cleanly in the middle of the landing pad.

'Ze best szump so far!' announced Baron de Couberpen. 'Cheetah, from ze penceel case of Bairt, is in ze lead!'

Bert's pencils all applauded Cheetah, but this time Cheetah didn't smile. He was sneering at Fleur, the next competitor.

Baron de Couberpen blew his whistle and

Fleur ran towards the jump. As she got closer to the jump line she slipped and slid a bit. She managed to regain her balance before her jump, but she didn't go very far, only just reaching the landing pad.

A gasp went around all the spectators (apart from Bert's pencils, Penny noticed).

'*Allors*. Fleur of ze penceel case of Ciara falls short, leaving Cheetah in ze lead!' proclaimed Baron de Couberpen before blowing his whistle for the next competitor.

It was Ernie's turn. He ran down the track even faster than Fleur. When he got to the same spot he lost his footing and took off at an angle. Somehow he managed to writhe in the air and land on the pad, only a little better than Fleur's jump and not as good as Cheetah's.

'Zat puts Airnee into ze final!' announced Baron de Couberpen before blowing his whistle for Lucy's pencil Stripes to take her turn. Both Stripes, and then Polly, seemed to skid as they came close to the jump line, but both landed safely on the landing pad, having jumped further than Fleur.

Then it was Penny's turn. All Ralph's pencils, as well as Smudge and Gloop, were cheering loudly for her. But Penny tried to block them out and focus on the run, especially the tricky bit at the end that everybody since Cheetah had slipped on.

Baron de Couberpen blew his whistle and Penny started towards the jump. Normally she would have been focusing only on the landing pad, but this time Penny was scanning the ground around the jump line. As she got closer she saw it – scatterings of slippery pencil shavings. They were the same colour as the carpet, so without looking out for them, she wouldn't have seen them. Penny managed to avoid all the pencil shavings and jumped. She landed even further than Cheetah, putting herself into the lead of the competition.

Ralph's pencils went crazy, running out of the

stands and crowding around Penny to pat her on the back. Penny tried to break free of them so that she could warn Mack about the pencil shavings, but Baron de Couberpen was already blowing his whistle and it was too late.

Mack sprinted down the track at full pace. If he didn't slow down and slipped on a shaving, he would really hurt himself. Penny half covered her eyes as Mack reached the jump line. But unlike all the others, he didn't slip or trip and made the longest jump of all!

Ralph's – and also Sarah's – pencils jumped up and down with glee.

'And zair we 'ave it,' said Baron de Couberpen. 'Our six Penceelympians. Representeeng ze penceel case of Ralph, Mack and Pennee!'

Ralph's pencils hosited Penny and Mack up onto their shoulders.

'Representeeng ze penceel case of Bairt: Cheetah!'

Bert's pencils made a sound like a pack of wild animals. Cheetah smiled smugly.

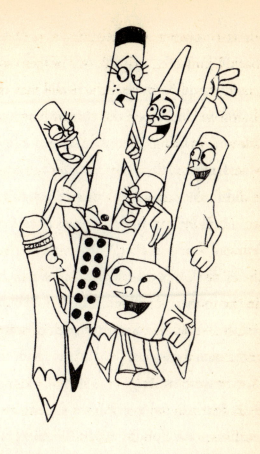

'Respresenteeng ze penceel case of Lucee: Stripes!'

All the pencils with Lucy Williams name labels clapped for joy. Stripes blushed so hard her white stripes disappeared and she looked like an ordinary red coloured pencil.

'In feefth place, representing ze penceel case of Sarah: Pollee!'

Sarah's pencils cheered excitedly, and Ralph's pencils joined in too. Even though her mind was on other things, Penny managed a few claps for her friend.

'And finallee, representeeng ze pencil case of Seán – 'oo I believe is also known as ze Chewair – Airnee!'

Seán the Chewer's misshapen pencils hoisted Ernie onto their shoulders. The whole bunch together looked like the aftermath of some horrific pencil case accident, apart from the fact that they were smiling.

'Ze next official event is ze Openeeng Ceremonee on Sunday night. Until zen, ze Penceelympians will train for ze two additional events, Roweeng and Archeree. But for today, we will finish class earlee. Enjoy your celebrations, and make sure you are back as ze children left you before zey return.'

And with that, all of the pencils took Baron de Couberpen's advice and went off to celebrate their team's performance in their pencil cases. All except for Penny, who managed to slip away from the celebrations unnoticed.

'Excuse me, Baron de Couberpen,' said Penny quietly. She'd never spoken to the Baron before, and found it quite intimidating.

'Ah. Pennee of ze penceel case of Ralph. An excellent perform-ance today. I do 'ope you're not tryeeng to bribe me,' said Baron de Couberpen, raising an eyebrow.

'Of course not,' said Penny. 'But I think the final few jumps – in fact all the jumps after Cheetah's – were sabotaged.'

'Yes, sabotage,' said Baron de Couberpen, drawing out the sound of the French word. 'A beautiful sounding word with a nasty meaning, no?'

'Erm,' said Penny, unsure how to answer.

'What makes you zink zey were sabotaged?' asked Baron de Couberpen.

'Come and see for yourself,' said Penny, leading Baron de Couberpen to the jump line. 'Someone put tiny little slippery bits of pencil shavings …'

Penny trailed off. The jump line was gone, and all of the pencil shavings were gone too.

'I do not see anee tinee, leetle, slipperee bits of penceel shaveengs,' said Baron de Couberpen. 'But eizer way, if everybodee is affected equallee, what is ze problem?'

Penny frowned.

'Run along and celebrate with all ze ozer penceels in ze penceel case of Ralph,' said Baron de Couberpen.

Realising there was nothing more she could do

to convince Baron de Couberpen that Cheetah
was a cheater, Penny went back to the pencil case.
As she was pulling the zip closed, something
on Bert's desk caught her eye. All Bert's pencils
were gathered around Bert's pencil case. And one

of them had a very clean foot, as though it had
been freshly sharpened. Penny looked closer, and
gasped. The pencil that the foot belonged to was
exactly the same colour as the carpet!

Certain that her suspicions about Cheetah were correct, Penny went to find Gloop.

Chapter 7

Archery

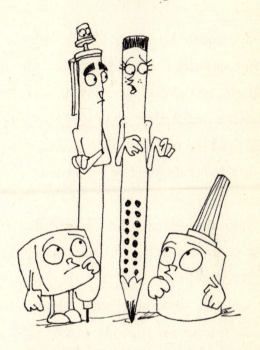

Penny, Gloop, Mack and Smudge were gathered in a corner of the pencil case, discussing Penny's suspicions.

'I don't know, Penny,' said Mack. 'I didn't notice any slippery bits when I ran down. Maybe the others were just nervous?'

'I don't think so,' said Penny. 'They were certainly there when I ran down. Maybe you got lucky and missed them. Your lead is finer than everyone else's.'

'And a recent *sharpening*,' said Smudge, lowering his voice and looking around the pencil case, 'would explain the clean sock on Bert's other pencil. Bert never sharpens his pencils. And the inside of his pencil case is so filthy the wood would be blackened instantly.'

'It certainly adds up,' said Gloop. 'Cheetah needed to do very well in the final heat to get into the competition.'

'So what do we do now?' asked Penny. 'Baron de Couberpen wasn't at all interested.'

'Hmmm,' said Gloop. 'Well, the first thing is for you two to be very careful during training and next week's competition,' he said to Penny and Mack. 'If Cheetah is willing to sabotage the competition in front of the whole class, then he'll stop at nothing to win.'

'There's one thing I don't get,' said Smudge. 'How did Cheetah manage to rig the scores?'

'Maybe he's not working alone,' suggested Mack.

'Any prizes for guessing who it might be?' said Penny, shuddering.

'You don't mean …' said Smudge.

'Black Texta,' said Penny. 'Why not? When things are going wrong he always seems to show up. And we know that he's in with Bert's pencils.'

'You could be right, Penny,' said Gloop. 'But how does that explain the changing of the scores? That wasn't texta, that was the chalk.'

'Maybe he's influencing them somehow. Hypnotising them with the smell of his ink or something,' said Penny.

'It wouldn't be the first time,' said Gloop, remembering the time Black Texta had overpowered him with stinky ink and kicked Penny out of the pencil case.

'How does he do it?' asked Mack.

'He just takes off his lid …' began Penny.

'No,' said Mack, shaking his head. 'How does he keep coming back? He's been expelled, confiscated, eaten by a lamp beast …'

'We don't know that he got eaten by the lamp beast,' said Gloop.

'Either way,' said Penny, 'when anything bad happens, Black Texta's usually behind it. And he just gets stronger and stronger.'

'Luckily with Baron de Couberpen's daily training, we're a bit stronger too,' said Mack. 'That Black Texta won't know what hit him if he takes us on this time!'

'Let's not worry about that too much at the moment,' said Gloop. 'You two have the Pencilympiad to focus on. It would mean the world to the coloured pencils if one of you was to win.'

'We'll do our best,' said Mack.

'One other thing,' said Gloop. 'We have to warn the other Pencilympians that they may be in danger.'

'Do I get to go undercover again?' asked Penny excitedly.

'No,' said Gloop. 'There shouldn't be any need for that. If you could just have a quiet word to them at training tomorrow, that should do the trick.'

When the children left the classroom for their Health class the next morning, Penny and Mack went with Polly, Stripes, Ernie and Cheater to meet Baron de Couberpen for their special training.

'I wonder what everybody else will be doing?' Polly said to Mack and Penny.

Suddenly a whistle blew. The pencils turned around to see Gloop standing

on Mrs Sword's desk with a whistle around his neck.

'*Gloop* is in charge!' said Penny, stunned that Gloop hadn't mentioned anything about it.

'Ze fat fellow seemed ze most responsible,' said Baron de Couberpen, who had overheard.

'Everybodee is 'ere. Good,' he continued. 'Zis morneeng we are going to learn Archeree.'

'Oh, goody!' said Ernie, who still couldn't believe his good fortune in qualifying for the Pencilympiad.

'Zis is ze most dangerous of all ze Penceelympic sports,' said Baron de Couberpen. 'It demands precision like no ozer. One mistake can be fatal.'

All the Pencilympians gasped.

'Zat is why I am only teacheeng it to you now – 'oo knows what kind of catastrophee we would 'ave 'ad on our 'ands if we'd let everybodee try it.'

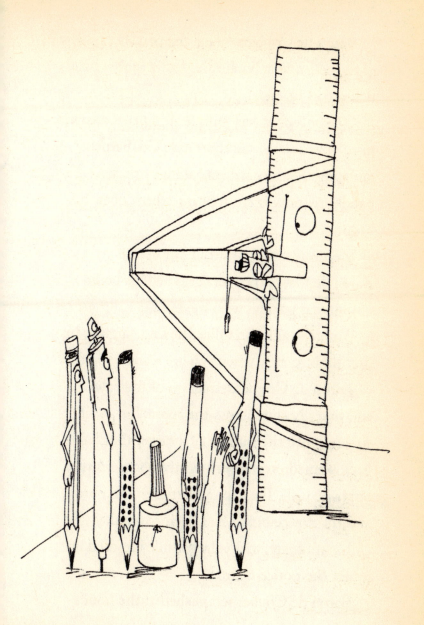

Baron de Couberpen led the pencils to a row of upright rulers. Each ruler had a rubber band tied across its ends.

'Ze concept is very simple. You place yourself in ze bow like so,' said Baron de Couberpen, grabbing the ruler halfway along with his hands and poking his foot into the rubber band.

'Zen you stretch yourself out like zis …' Baron de Couberpen straightened his body until it was parallel with the floor.

'You take aim carefullee,' he said, jiggling his foot slightly, 'zen, when you are readee, you fire!'

Baron de Couberpen let go of the ruler and literally shot across the room, his point sticking into the middle of a target that had been pinned on the cork notice board on the opposite wall. The ground between the bow and the notice board had been covered by the children's coats, with a larger pile bundled up under the notice board.

Baron de Couberpen pushed at the notice

board with his hands to free his point, and
dropped safely onto the pile of coats below.

'Zis is not wide enough!' he yelled at
the pieces of chalk who were arranging
the children's coats on the ground. 'Zey are
beginnairs! Zey could fly off in anee direction!'

'Sorry Baron,' said the pieces of chalk,
spreading the coats a lot wider.

'Now,' he said. 'As it is your first attempt, we
will do zis one at a time. Let's begin with ze
'ighest point scorair, Mack from ze pencil case
of Ralph.'

Mack stepped forward and grabbed hold
of the ruler. He placed his foot in the rubber
band and tried to straighten up. But it was
very difficult and he wobbled unsteadily before
shooting off straight into the floor in front of
him.

'Better luck next time,' said Baron de
Couberpen. 'Next!'

Reluctantly Penny went up to have her
turn. Like Mack she found it very difficult to

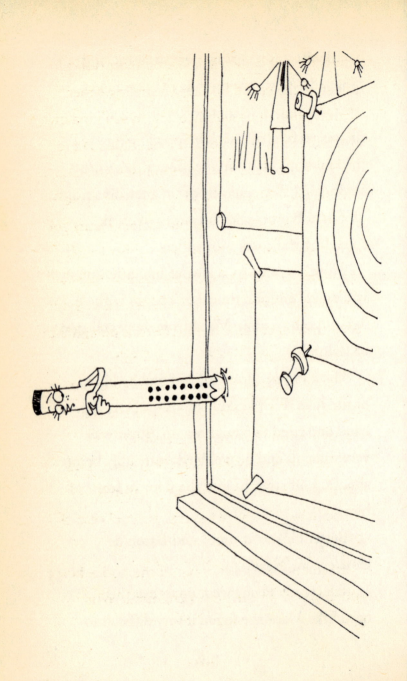

straighten her body out, and even more difficult to aim at the target. She kept wobbling either slightly above it or slightly below it, in a kind of rhythm. Penny counted how long it took her to wobble from above the target to below the target. Five seconds. She started wobbling back up again. Another five seconds. This time, when Penny got to two and a half, she let go. The rubber band thrust her forwards towards the cork board at a frightening speed. Penny shut her eyes and didn't open them again until she felt her toe plough into the notice board, wedging her in firmly.

Penny looked around her. She was inches away from the wooden border and about as far away from the target as possible.

'Zat was exceptionell for a beginnair,' said Baron de Couberpen. 'You are a naturell, Mademoiselle Pennee from ze penceel case of Ralph.'

Penny pulled her foot out of the notice board and dropped on the pile of children's coats below.

Polly, Stripes, Cheetah and Ernie had mixed success in their attempts. Ernie aimed so badly that he sailed straight up, hit the roof, and landed exactly where he had begun. Polly did the best, managing to hit the very edge of the target. Stripes actually got her lead stuck in the roof, and had to be saved by a blackboard duster. Cheetah also did quite well, missing the cork board, and getting stuck in the wall.

While Penny and Polly waited in line, Penny turned to her friend and told her all about the conversation between herself, Gloop, Mack and Smudge.

'I thought there was something funny about the ground near the long jump yesterday,' Polly said. 'But I didn't say anything because nobody else complained.'

'I tried to complain to Baron de Couberpen, but he wouldn't listen,' said Penny.

'I think you're right about Cheetah. Plus, he hasn't been the friendliest this morning.'

It was true. While all the other pencils had helped each other with the Archery, Cheetah had stood off to one side, looking at them scornfully.

'The lesson's nearly over. Mack's chatting to Ernie now. Can you have a word to Stripes when – I mean if – she gets back?' said Penny.

Stripes had just had her second fling, and she was wedged in the gap between the wall and the ceiling.

'Mush bettair zan last time,' encouraged Baron de Couberpen, as the blackboard dusters tried to free Stripes from her latest predicament.

The pencils practised for the rest of the morning lesson, and by the end all of them were flying quite straight, even if they didn't fly quite far enough to reach the target.

'Zat was excellon,' said Baron de Couberpen when practice was over and the sound of the children's footsteps could be heard in the corridor. 'Tomorrow we will be practiseeng Roweeng.'

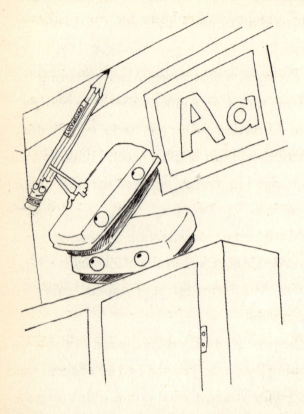

The pencils hurried back to their pencil cases as the chalk and blackboard dusters put the children's coats away. Polly hopped into Ralph's pencil case with Penny and Mack to discuss how the plan had worked.

'Stripes wouldn't listen,' said Polly. 'You know what she's like. If it's not written on a label attached to her body, she won't believe it.'

'Ernie believed me,' said Mack. 'He's been terrorised by Seán the Chewer all his life, so he's used to looking around carefully, and he thought Cheetah was up to something too.'

'Good,' said Penny. 'Well, at the very least, everyone's been warned, whether or not they choose to believe us.'

'Not everyone's been warned,' said Gloop.

'Eh?' said Penny, Mack and Polly together.

'Nobody's told Cheetah,' said Gloop.

'But … But … He doesn't need to be told,' spluttered Penny. 'He's the one doing the cheating!'

'Maybe he's been hypnotised,' suggested Gloop.

'It is a noble suggestion, but I don't think so,' said Polly. 'I've been watching Cheetah, and he knows exactly what he's doing.'

'Okay,' said Gloop, putting up his hands. 'It was just a possibility I thought we should consider. But if you're sure …'

'We're absolutely positive,' said Penny.

Polly and Mack nodded.

'Alright then,' said Gloop. 'Let's all be very careful. I don't know exactly what it is Black Texta wants, but I know he'll stop at nothing to get it.'

Chapter 8

Detention

When Mrs Payne came back to the classroom after the morning's Health class, she blew her whistle so loudly that the glass in the windows rattled and threatened to break.

'Who is responsible for THIS?' she shrieked.

The children turned their heads to the spot that Mrs Payne was pointing to on the wall, exactly where Stripes had been stuck between the wall and the ceiling. In their attempts to rescue her, the blackboard dusters had left several large, colourful chalk marks.

'They weren't there when we left the classroom this morning, which means one of you skipped my exercise class to put them there!' Mrs Payne boomed. 'As if being untidy wasn't bad enough. Who was it?' shouted Mrs Payne, her beady eyes singling out every child in the class and making them shake in their shoes.

'Not going to own up, eh?' yelled Mrs Payne. 'If there's one thing I can't stand more than a vandal, it's a vandal who skips class! And I have a way of checking who it was.'

Mrs Payne went to the SHAMPERS chart on the wall.

'I'll just see which of you has done less exercise today than they should have, and that

will tell me who was missing from class,' she
boomed. 'This is your last chance. If you own up
now, your punishment will be considerably less
than if I have to work it out.'

The children remained silent, looking around
the class to see if they could spot the guilty party.

'Right,' yelled Mrs Payne. 'I did warn you.'

Mrs Payne turned away from the class to add up the exercises. The children in the front row craned their necks to see if they could see what she was writing on the chart. Five minutes later, Mrs Payne turned to face the class again.

'Well, it seems we have a new leader, because RALPH didn't do his laps today!'

'What?' said Ralph, accidentally out loud.

'A vandal, a liar, and a rude boy who talks out of turn in class!' yelled Mrs Payne.

'But I did do my laps. I wrote them on the sheet ...' began Ralph.

'Silence!' bellowed Mrs Payne. 'What did I just say about talking out of turn in class?'

Ralph sat very quietly, unsure whether he was supposed to answer or not.

The recess bell rang. None of the children moved.

'You may all go,' shouted Mrs Payne. 'Except for Ralph.'

All the children got up and got their lunch, those with cake trying to smuggle it out under their jumpers. But they could have waved it in front of Mrs Payne's face today and she wouldn't have noticed. She was too busy glaring at Ralph.

When all of the children had left the class, except two who were seated next to each other, Mrs Payne took her eyes off Ralph and glared at Sarah.

'What are you still doing here?' she roared.

'Mrs Payne, Ralph didn't skip Health class today,' said Sarah bravely.

'You're going to confess to save your little friend, are you?' Mrs Payne yelled.

'No. He's my exercise partner and we were together the whole time,' said Sarah.

'So you were in it together?' blared Mrs Payne.

'No,' protested Ralph. 'We were in class the whole time ...'

Ralph trailed off as Mrs Payne's face changed colour from an angry red to a deep purple.

'May I offer a suggestion, Mrs Payne?' said Sarah, just loud enough to be heard.

'Very well then,' screeched Mrs Payne.

'Check his hands,' said Sarah.

'What?!' said Mrs Payne.

'Check his hands,' repeated Sarah. 'If he was throwing the dusters at the ceiling, he'd have chalk on his hands.'

Mrs Payne glared at Sarah for a moment longer, then snapped her head at Ralph.

'Hands on the table, boy. Palms up!' she ordered.

Ralph did exactly as he was told.

Mrs Payne examined his hands. There wasn't a trace of chalk anywhere.

'So you washed them, eh?' she snorted.

'Check his sleeves, check his pants. It's harder to get chalk dust out of clothing,' suggested Sarah.

Mrs Payne hauled Ralph up out of his seat by the scruff of his neck. She examined his clothes roughly, but found no chalk dust. She

let go of Ralph and he dropped back into his
seat.

'You appear to be clean,' shouted Mrs Payne.
Then she turned to Sarah.

'And you …' Mrs Payne said quietly. 'The military could do with people like you,' she continued at normal volume. 'Keen minds. We're not only about soldiering.'

Sarah looked at Ralph and raised her eyebrows.

'From the evidence presented today, I find the accused not guilty,' shouted Mrs Payne. 'You are both free to go.'

Ralph and Sarah quickly got up out of their chairs and left the classroom before Mrs Payne had a chance to change her mind.

'Thanks for that, Sarah,' said Ralph, breathing a sigh of relief.

'There's still one thing that's not clear,' said Sarah. 'You ran more laps than normal today, and on Mrs Payne's sheet it said you had run less.'

'Maybe she added up wrong,' said Ralph, shrugging.

'Or maybe the person who put those marks on the ceiling did it on purpose to get you into

trouble,' said Sarah, looking across the playground with narrowed eyes at Bert, who was terrorising a group of children from first class.

'But why would he do that, other than the obvious?' said Ralph.

'It could be because you stuck up for me yesterday,' said Sarah thoughtfully. 'Or more likely, he wants to be the class champion, which would explain why he changed your score.'

'But that still doesn't explain the chalk on the ceiling,' said Ralph.

'No, it doesn't,' said Sarah.

'And honestly,' said Ralph, 'I don't think Bert is capable of thinking that far in advance.'

'Hmmm,' said Sarah. 'But either way, he seems very keen to win the competition, and since you're the one stopping him, you'd better be more careful than normal.'

Chapter 9

Penny's Reward

The next morning, Baron de Couberpen took Penny, Polly, Mack, Ernie, Stripes and Cheetah out to the playground to teach them how to row. The children exercised in the top playground, so Baron de Couberpen and the pencils went to the drinking fountains in the bottom playground.

The pieces of chalk had already prepared the rowing course for the pencils. They had blocked

up the plughole in the trough with an old
handkerchief, so the trough was full of water.
Floating in the water were some old drink
bottle lids, with paddle pop sticks on
either side.

'Zis morneeng, we will learn roweeng.' As
anybodee been roweeng before?' asked Baron de
Couberpen.

All the pencils shook their heads.

'It is veree easee,' said Baron de Couberpen.
'Ze onlee difficultee is zat you do ze race facing
backwards. Choose a boat, and 'op in.'

The pencils climbed up to the trough. Just
as Polly was about to hop into the nearest boat,
Cheetah came barging through and almost
knocked poor Polly into the water!

'Watch what you're doing, Cheetah,' said
Mack.

'What are you going to do about it?' sneered
Cheetah.

'Oh, ho ho!' said Baron de Couberpen. 'I see
zair is alreadee friendlee rivalree!'

'Not exactly,' muttered Mack, hopping into the last boat.

As rowing wasn't quite as dangerous as archery, the pencils were allowed to practise all together. This wasn't really the best idea, as they weren't very good, and kept bumping into each other. Penny noticed that whenever Cheetah bumped into her it was always a lot harder than anyone else. The only thing to do to avoid him was to get into a position where she could see Cheetah. Since they were rowing backwards, that meant getting in front of him.

Once Penny overtook Cheetah she found rowing much easier. She was in the lead, and could see how all the other pencils were doing. Ernie still hadn't got the hang of it and was veering too far to the right, then over-correcting and going too far to the left. Mack was doing worse and spinning around in circles. He had gone a funny shade of green and was looking decidedly seasick.

Polly, on the other hand, was doing quite well, and soon rowed up next to Penny.

'This is quite fun, isn't it?' said Polly.

'Uh-oh. Watch out!' said Penny.

Cheetah had spotted them and was making a bee-line towards them.

'Come on, Penny! Row!' called Polly.

Penny and Polly rowed as hard as they could, and managed to escape from Cheetah.

They reached the other end of the trough and prepared to moor their boats.

'What are you doeeng?' said Baron de Couberpen. 'Ze lesson isn't even half ovair! Row back ze ozair way.'

Penny and Polly looked at each other. Rowing the other way meant they would have to pass Cheetah, and they knew he'd be aiming for them.

'Psst, Polly,' said Penny. 'Let's split up. You go right, and I'll go left. Then he'll have to choose one of us.'

'Okay,' said Polly, casting off and rowing to her right.

'What are you doing?' asked Penny, as Polly nearly crashed into her.

'I'm rowing to the right,' said Polly, turning around and seeing Cheetah closing in.

'But we're going backwards, so right means left!' said Penny in a panic.

Cheetah was very close now, and about to ram them.

'Just go!' said Polly.

Cheetah was so close that the pencils could only row parallel to the end of the trough to escape. Penny took three hard strokes and managed to move her boat out of the way in time. Polly did the same, and instead of hitting them, Cheetah rowed through the gap in the middle and ploughed into the bank at the end of the trough. The bow of his boat hit the edge and stopped. The rest of the boat kept going, flipping up in the air and flinging Cheetah into the water.

'Help! Help! I can't swim!' cried Cheetah as he bobbed up and down on the surface of the water.

Penny and Polly looked at each other, then Penny turned her boat around and started rowing towards Cheetah.

'What are you doing?' cried Polly.

'We can't let him drown,' said Penny.

When Penny got close enough to Cheetah, she held her oar out to him.

'Grab hold of this,' she said.

Cheetah clung to the oar and Penny hoisted him out of the water and onto her boat.

'*Tres bien! Tres bien!*' said Baron de Couberpen, clapping from the shore. 'A wonderful display of true sportspenceelship.'

Cheetah sneered weakly at Penny as she rowed him towards the shore.

'It's all your fault. If you hadn't moved your boat ...' he said.

'You're most welcome, Cheetah,' said
Penny. 'Now get out of my boat, and out of
my sight.'

Penny deposited the shivering Cheetah on
the bank, and rowed back down the trough.

When training was over, Baron de Couberpen
sent the pencils back to the classroom, but
asked Penny to stay behind. Penny was hoping
he was going to say something
about Cheetah's cheating, but
what he actually said took her
completely by surprise.

'Zat was very 'eroic, what
you did today, Penny of ze
penceel case of Ralph,' said
Baron de Couberpen.

'Thank you, Baron,' said
Penny.

'In a time of war, such
braveree would be rewarded
with a Graphite Cross!'

Penny's eyes lit up

at the mention of the greatest medal for bravery for pencilkind.

'Unfortunatelee, or rathair fortunatelee,' continued Baron de Couberpen, 'we are not at war. But zair is somezeeng I can offair you as a reward …'

Baron de Couberpen whispered his proposal to Penny.

'I accept!' said Penny.

'But you are not to tell anybodee. It is to be a surprise!' cautioned Baron de Couberpen.

'My lips are sealed,' said Penny, and she bounded off happily back to Ralph's pencil case.

Chapter 10

The Opening Ceremony

The rest of the week in the lead-up to the
Pencilympics went by in a blur for Penny. Not
only did she have all the training, plus preparing
for her secret reward, but Mrs Sword was giving
the children some new, exciting work to do.

The schoolwork wasn't really maths, and
wasn't really drawing, but a mixture of the

two, and it involved a new kind of drawing implement.

Penny first met the new implement after lunch on the day she'd started rowing. The new implement was silver, like Penny, but very shiny. She had two legs, one was long and skinny, and the other was shorter with a big, hollow hoop on the end.

'Hello,' said the new implement. 'I'm Mariko.'

'I'm Penny,' said Penny, looking at the new implement with interest. 'Would it be rude to ask what you do?'

'Not at all,' said Mariko. 'I'm a drawing compass. I help children, and pencils like you of course, draw perfect circles.'

'So you're a kind of teacher ...' said Penny, as Ralph picked her up.

'No,' said Mariko.

Penny suddenly realised that Mariko was getting very close to her. Ralph was unscrewing something on the side of Mariko's hoop, and

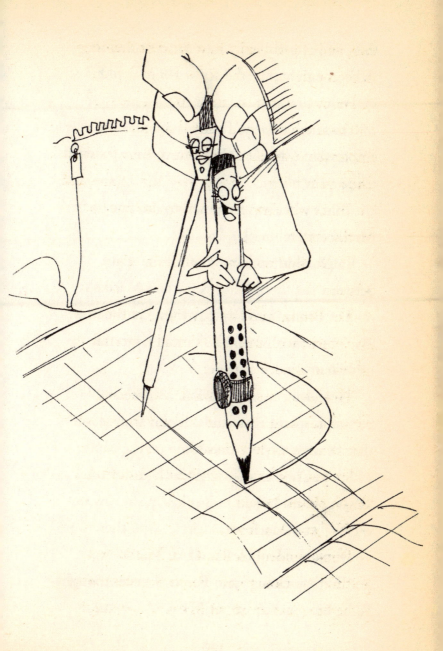

then he popped Penny into the centre of it! When he tightened the screw Penny couldn't move.

'I'm terribly sorry,' Penny laughed, a little embarrassed, 'but Ralph seems to have fastened me to your hoop.'

'That's what he's supposed to do,' said Mariko, stretching her legs out.

Ralph adjusted Mariko until the space between the tip of Penny's toe and Mariko's other foot measured exactly three centimetres. Then he poked Mariko's sharp leg into the middle of a piece of paper.

'Here, we go,' said Mariko. 'Wheeeeeee!'

Ralph spun Penny and Mariko around, so that Penny's toe left a neat line on the paper, which finished exactly where it had started. When Penny looked more closely, she saw it wasn't just a line, it was a circle! And there were no wiggles or wobbles at all.

'That's amazing!' said Penny. 'I never thought I'd be able to draw so well!'

Penny and Mariko spent the class drawing circles of different sizes. Every so often Ralph would make adjustments so that Mariko's legs stretched further apart or closer together, to make bigger or smaller circles.

When the bell rang, Ralph unscrewed Penny and pulled her out of Mariko's hoop.

'Oh, goody,' said Penny. 'I can't wait to introduce you to everyone!'

'I can't,' said Mariko.

'What?' said Penny.

'I can't come with you. I have to go in the special Maths Set case.'

'But why?' asked Penny.

'My toe. It's too sharp. It's too dangerous to go in a normal pencil case.'

And before they could say goodbye properly, Ralph put Mariko in her special case and Penny back in his regular pencil case.

As Ralph and his classmates were still under ten, they didn't have any weekend homework, so all the children left their pencil cases at school over the weekend. Most of the pencils disliked the weekend, as they didn't get a chance to draw or write. But this weekend was different, as Sunday night was the Pencilympic Opening Ceremony.

While the Pencilympians were busy doing their last-minute training, the rest of the writing implements were designing their team flags or helping out with the decorations. Baron de Couberpen was bustling about, giving instructions, as well as coaching the athletes.

'No, no, no!' he kept saying. 'Not like zat, like zis!'

All in all the Pencilympians thought Baron de Couberpen was a lot more nervous than they were.

Finally, Sunday evening arrived and it was time for the opening ceremony. The writing implements all lined up in their teams outside the Pencilympic Stadium. Ciara's and Malcolm's pencils, along with those of the other children in the class whose pencils didn't qualify, were inside counting down to the start of the ceremony.

'Ten, nine, eight …'
Penny looked
around at
the flags
fluttering
in the breeze.
Even if she
hadn't been
told that they had to line up in
alphabetical order based on the first
letter of their owner's name, Penny
would have easily been able to pick
out each team by the design on its flag.
'… seven, six, five …'
At the front was Bert's team. The
flag was mainly black, with a skull and
crossbones in the middle of it. Next was
a flag with a slice of cream cake on it for
Lucy's team. Then Ralph's team, with the red
racing car. Just behind was Sarah's team, who
had drawn lots of glittery stars and a crescent
moon on a blue background. And last was a

135

green flag with big, white teeth on it for Seán the Chewer.

'... four, three, two, one!'

Bert's pencils, lead by Cheetah, marched into the stadium, carrying their flag. The pencils seated in the stadium all cheered just as loudly for Bert's pencils as they had for their own team mates during the qualification.

Next it was Lucy's team. Stripes carried the flag into the stadium to even louder cheers from the crowds of pencils.

Then it was Penny's turn. She and Mack carried the flag with one arm each. As they entered the stadium the roar of the crowd was deafening – even louder than Mrs Payne's normal speaking voice! Penny had never felt so proud to be a part of Ralph's pencil case, and to be sharing the moment with her best friend Mack was very special indeed.

Ralph's pencils all gathered in a little spot in the centre, as Sarah's pencils came in. Polly carried the flag through the entrance way and Penny broke into applause with the rest of the pencils. In fact, because they were such good friends with Sarah's pencils, Ralph's writing

implements made more noise than the other pencils in the stadium put together!

When Sarah's pencils had settled into their seats, Ernie entered the stadium carrying the flag for Seán the Chewer's team. The pencils in the stadium clapped even louder than ever, very proud of the brave little team who lived in constant fear of being chewed – which, second only to sharpening, was every pencil's worst nightmare!

Then everyone went quiet as Baron de Couberpen stood at the microphone.

'Good eveneeng, fellow penceels and writeeng implements. It is with great pleasure that I declare ze games of ze Penceelympiad open!'

All the pencils cheered and threw streamers.

'I would like to welcome to ze stage, a penceel 'oo will take ze Penceelympic Oath on be'alf of all ze Penceelympians. Zis penceel 'as shown amazeeng courage, dedication to 'er team mates, and to 'er sport. From the pencil case of Ralph, Pennee!'

All the pencils in the stadium cheered even louder than ever for Penny. As she walked to the stage, she found it very daunting. Of course, Penny had been the centre of attention before, but only in front of Ralph's, and sometimes Sarah's, pencils. But in front of the pencils from the whole class it was very different.

Penny passed by Bert's pencils, who instead of cheering were booing, but only loudly enough for Penny to hear. Penny ignored them as she climbed the stairs. She had something special planned for them later.

Baron de Couberpen passed the microphone to Penny.

'On behalf of all pencils taking part in classroom 3B's Pencilympic Games,' began Penny, 'I promise to respect the rules of fair play,' she continued, staring hard at Cheetah, 'sportspencilship, without doping, for the glory of sport and the honour of my pencil case.'

All the pencils cheered, and even Cheetah

seemed to be smiling as Penny walked back to
her team.

Then it was time to light the Pencilympic
Flame. Two pieces of chalk carried in a
magnifying glass while another piece unveiled
the Pencilympic Cauldron, which was a
khaki-coloured spiral candle. The two pieces
of chalk with the magnifying glass held it so
that the moonlight was focused on the wick of
the candle. Within seconds, the wick started

smoking, then it burst into flame. All the pencils cheered even louder than ever.

Baron de Couberpen came back to the microphone.

'Tonight is a night for celebration, but to our Penceelympians. Do not partee too 'ard. Ze next five days will not be easy, and you will 'ave to perform at your best everee second. But I promise you, ze more you concentrate zis week, ze more you will enjoy ze closeeng ceremonee on Friday night. Let us meet again tomorrow morneeng for ze 'undred centimetair sprint. Goodnight!'

Chapter 11

One Hundred Centimetre Sprint

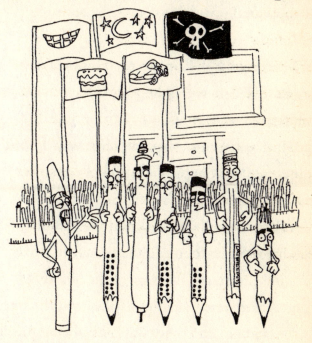

The first day of the Pencilympiad dawned bright and early. Penny and Mack were woken up with breakfast in bed by Gloop, Smudge and all the coloured pencils.

'Oh, no. I'm so nervous I couldn't eat a thing,' said Mack.

'You should at least try a bite. You'll need your strength,' said Gloop. 'Not to mention that all the coloured pencils will be very disappointed if you don't eat it,' he added in a whisper.

Mack took one dainty bite of his breakfast. It was so delicious that he wolfed the rest down and started on Penny's.

'Hey!' said Penny, slapping him away. 'I don't think the Pencilympic Oath allows you to eat another Pencilympian's breakfast.'

When the bell sounded, and the children had left the classroom, all the pencils hurried to the sprint track. The flags of the different pencil cases were flying on flag poles at the top of the stadium and there was music being piped through a loud speaker. The atmosphere was fantastic.

'Good luck, Penny. Good luck, Mack,' said Amber and Jade. 'We'll be watching you very closely.'

And instead of joining the rest of Ralph's

pencils in the stand, Amber and Jade
disappeared inside a small commentary box
near the finish line.

'Everybodee 'ere?' said Baron de Couberpen,
ticking off names against his marshalling list.
'Okay. Pennee, since you were ze winnair at
qualifyeeng, you are in lane one. Mack, lane two.
Pollee, lane three. Cheetah, lane four. Stripes,
lane five. Airnee, lane six.'

The pencils got into their lanes and into the starting blocks.

'The ground feels a bit sticky,' said Penny.

'Yeah,' said Mack.

'I think so too,' said Polly. 'And it smells a little like …'

'On your marks!' said Baron de Couberpen, his voice echoing over the loud speaker. 'Get set – and go!'

'And they're off and running!' said Jade's voice, magically broadcast over the loud speaker.

'Well, some of them are off and running,' said Amber's voice, joining Jade's. 'It looks like Penny, Mack and Polly are having trouble getting out of the starting blocks!'

'And Ernie hits the lead!' said Jade. 'He was the slowest of the Pencilympians to qualify in the sprint, but he's running rings around them today.'

'Next is Stripes!' said Amber. 'Followed closely by Cheetah, and finally Penny, Mack and Polly several centimetres behind!'

'And look at Ernie go!' said Jade. 'There's nothing holding him back today.'

'Who would have thought a pencil with a head that shape could be so aerodynamic?' said Amber.

'And he crosses the finish line! The first event

in the Pencilympics goes to Ernie, followed by Stripes, Cheetah, oh, and a three-way tie for last between Penny, Mack and Polly,' finished Jade, as Amber rushed down from the commentary booth to interview Ernie.

'So Ernie, how does it feel to have won this history-making race? Did you think you could do it?' asked Amber, thrusting a microphone in Ernie's face.

'Well,' said Ernie, trying to get his breath back, 'I just imagined that Seán the Chewer's hand was behind me. He was pretty hungry last week, so I had lots of practice running away.'

'And Stripes – congratulations on coming second. Was it a surprise?'

asked Amber, turning her attention, and the microphone, to Stripes.

'I've been training hard, watching my diet carefully, so not a surprise,' said Stripes matter-of-factly.

'And Cheetah, are you happy with your performance?' asked Amber.

'I would have preferred to come first,' said Cheetah, 'but at least I didn't come last,' he finished, sneering at Penny, Polly and Mack.

'And you three,' said Amber, turning to the pencils that came in fourth place. 'On form you should have come first, second and third. What went wrong?'

Penny was about to reply when Polly butted in.

'They just ran a better race today,' she said, smiling.

'Thank you, Polly,' said Amber, turning to face the crowd. 'This is Amber, reporting trackside. Now, back to Jade in the commentary booth.'

'Thank you, Amber,' said Jade. 'Join us again tomorrow for the High Jump, where we'll see if favourite Mack can rise to the same heights as in the qualifying round.'

'Why didn't you let Penny say anything about the stickiness?' Mack asked Polly on their way back to Ralph and Sarah's pencil cases.

'The race was over by then,' said Polly. 'It just would have sounded like sour grapes.'

'It's a bit of a coincidence that we were the favourites and our lanes smelt and felt like glue,' grumbled Penny.

'Well there's no use complaining about it,' said Polly. 'Baron de Couberpen wasn't interested last time you tried to warn him about cheating. Plus, we don't know for sure that the others' lanes didn't have glue, or whatever it was, in them either.'

'There's no point asking Cheetah or Stripes, and it would be downright mean to ask Ernie about it. It'd be like saying he didn't deserve to win,' said Penny.

'Whatever it was,' said Gloop, who had been listening in to the pencils' conversation for quite some time, 'you've got to put it out of your minds and focus on the remaining four events. And the tiny little matter of Ralph and Sarah's schoolwork.'

That afternoon, the children had another of the strange maths drawing classes. Ralph was drawing circles again, but this time, instead of

using Mariko to help, he was tying pieces of itchy, carpet-coloured string around Penny's waist, holding one end on the paper and whirling Penny around like a totem tennis ball.

The problem was, unlike her spins with Mariko, Penny didn't always end up at the exact spot from where she'd started, so Ralph's circles looked a bit like snails.

Behind Ralph, Bert was doing the same thing, but instead of getting frustrated with his owner, Cheetah was smiling to himself. At the end of the lesson, Cheetah made sure that Bert put him back in his pencil case without untying the carpet-coloured string from around his waist.

Chapter 12

High Jump

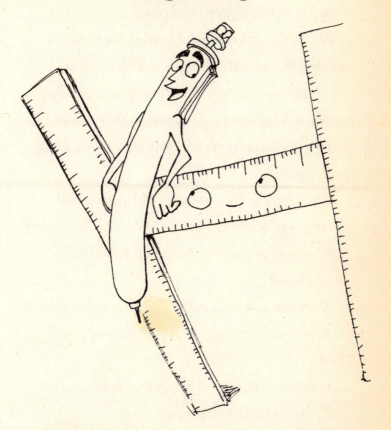

The mood in Ralph's pencil case on the second morning of the Pencilympiad was a lot more subdued than the previous day. The coloured pencils were very disappointed that neither Mack nor Penny had done very well, and although Mack was the favourite for the High Jump, they didn't have much confidence in him.

When the children went outside for their morning Health class, Ralph's pencils climbed out of the pencil case with little enthusiasm. Only Amber and Jade seemed excited, as they would get to report on everything from the commentary booth again.

Bert's pencils were nearby, whispering and looking very self-satisfied.

'What do you think they're up to today?' asked Penny.

'They can hardly sabotage the track this time, because everybody uses the same run-up,' said Mack.

'It didn't make any difference in the qualifying,' said Penny ruefully.

'Don't you worry about it,' said Gloop. 'I'll keep a close eye on them, and let Baron de Couberpen know at the first sign of foul play.'

Penny and Mack went to the start line where Baron de Couberpen was putting everybody in order. Even with his strange accent, it was hard to hear him above the cheering of the crowd and Jade and Amber's commentary.

'… surprising start to the competition with Ernie from Seán the Chewer's pencil case in the lead,' said Jade, 'followed by Stripes from Lucy Williams' pencil case and Cheetah, owned by Bert the Bully.'

'The inside word is that the pencils from Ralph and Sarah's pencil cases had problems with the track yesterday,' said Amber.

'Let's hope they can do a little better today,' said Jade.

'The format of today's competition is a little different from qualifying,' said Amber. 'Rather than having one jump each, the pencils will jump over a bar that will get higher and higher, until only one pencil remains. That pencil will be the winner.'

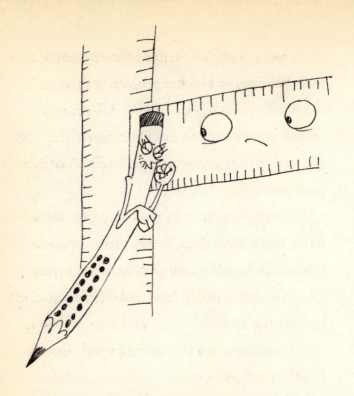

'And here comes Mack, going for a height of ten centimetres. His run-up looks good, he's left the ground, he's done it!'

'Now it's Ernie's turn. Of course, he's barely ten centimetres tall, but that didn't stop him coming second in qualification,' said Amber. 'He jumps … he clears!'

In the third round, at a height of thirty centimetres, things began to get interesting.

Both Ernie and Polly failed to clear the bar and were knocked out of the competition. Then in the fourth round, Penny was so busy keeping an eye on Cheetah that she mistimed her jump and instead of sailing over the bar, hit her head painfully on it instead.

'And at a height of forty centimetres we're down to the final three competitors,' said Amber. 'Mack, the favourite, and Stripes and Cheetah, who of course came second and third yesterday.'

'There goes Mack now,' said Jade, as Mack began his run-up. 'He's looking good, and oh, no! He's tripped!'

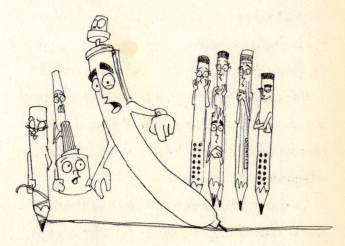

Mack hadn't seen the little blue string the same colour as the carpet that two of Bert's pencils had laid across the track, and didn't notice them pull it tight to make him trip. Even Gloop – who was watching very carefully – didn't notice the string.

All Mack knew was that one moment he was running on his foot, and the next the ground was coming towards his head at an alarming rate. He landed head-first on his clicker, which poked in then propelled him upwards and high over the bar.

'Hooray for Mack!' said Amber. 'He's really raised the bar this morning!'

'Is that a legal move?' asked Jade.

'Baron de Couberpen's consulting his rule book … and the answer is … the jump is good!'

'It's a whole new level of competition now,' said Jade.

'Here comes Stripes,' said Amber. 'She leaps, she's over – but oh, no! She's brought the bar down with her.'

'So Stripes is out of the High Jump,' said Jade.

'Now it's down to the last competitor, Cheetah,' said Amber. 'If he makes this jump, he and Mack will go on to fifty centimetres. If he doesn't, Mack will be the winner.'

'Cheetah takes his run-up … he jumps … he misses! He doesn't even get close! Mack has won! Mack has won!' screamed Jade with excitement.

All of Ralph's pencils ran out of the stands and clustered around Mack to congratulate him.

'And we'll see you all tomorrow, same time, same place – and hopefully same result – for the Long Jump,' said Amber.

'This is Jade and Amber, signing off,' said Jade, as she and Amber left the commentary booth to join the celebration with the rest of Ralph's pencils.

The party kept going all through recess, lunchtime and afternoon classes. Only when school had finished for the day did Penny, Smudge and Gloop get a chance to speak with Mack alone.

'What happened out there?' asked Penny.

'Everything was going fine, then I tripped,' said Mack.

'And he landed quite hard!' said Little Mack, poking out from under Mack's clicker with a black eye.

'What did you trip on?' asked Smudge.

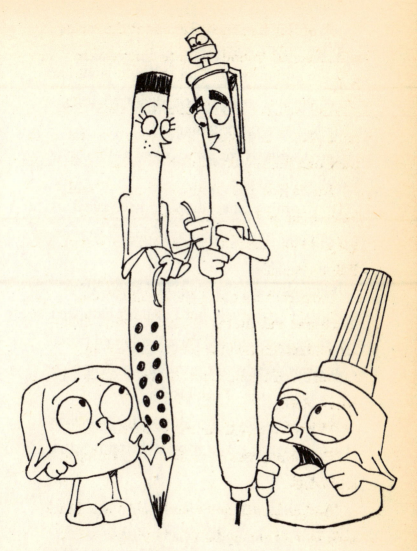

Penny looked closely at Mack's lead. She
picked up what looked like a little blue thread.

'What's that?' asked Gloop.

'If I'm not mistaken,' said Penny, 'it looks like a bit of the blue string the children were using in Maths Drawing yesterday.'

'And it's exactly the same colour as the carpet!' said Smudge.

'Do you think Cheetah might have asked Bert's pencils to trip Mack up, Gloop?' Penny asked.

'It wouldn't surprise me,' said Gloop. 'I was watching pretty closely, but I couldn't have seen something that thin and carpet-coloured from so far away. Were you tripped up too, Penny?'

'No,' said Penny. 'I just blew it.'

'Well,' said Gloop. 'It's obvious that Cheetah is up to something. You two had better be extra-careful tomorrow.'

Chapter 13

The Banned Substance

Ralph's coloured pencils were in such a good
mood all that night and the next morning that
it was impossible for Penny and Mack to worry
too much about Cheetah and what evils he
might have planned for them.

After Ralph had finished his homework, Penny and Mack had a chance to practise their long jumping skills. Both of them were doing even better than they had in the qualification round, and were feeling very confident about the third event of the Pencilympics.

'Welcome to another day of Pencilympic competition!' said Jade from the commentary booth.

'As the Pencilympians warm up for their third event, the long jump, let's have a quick recap of the overall score,' said Amber.

'At the moment, with two second places in the Sprint and the High Jump, Stripes from Lucy's pencil case is winning with four points!' said Jade.

All Lucy's pencils clapped and cheered for Stripes, who gave them a big wave.

'We have a three-way tie for second place between Ernie, who won the Sprint' – all Seán's pencils cheered loudly – 'Mack, who won the

High Jump' – Ralph's pencils jumped up and down in excitement – 'and Cheetah, who came third in the Sprint and equal second in the High Jump!'

Bert's pencils made lots of whooping noises that made the pencils next to them in the crowd feel a little frightened.

'The only pencil case without points on the board is Sarah's, so let's see if Polly can make an improvement today,' said Amber.

'Mack jumped the longest distance in the qualification round so he's the favourite again today,' said Jade.

'He's got a lot of spring in his step, and in his head!' said Amber, making all the spectators laugh.

'Baron de Couberpen is blowing his whistle, and Stripes is off!' said Jade.

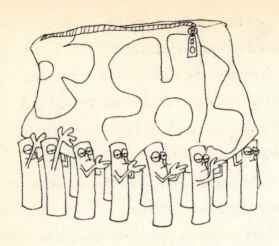

Stripes ran down the track even faster than she had in the Sprint. When she got to the jump line she leapt up gracefully and soared through the air, landing over half-way along the landing pad.

'And it's a brilliant jump!' said Amber.

'Of course, Stripes did the shortest jump of all the Pencilympians in the qualification round, so this is most unexpected …' began Jade.

'What's that?' interrupted Amber.

Some pieces of chalk had entered the stadium carrying …

'Is that Lucy's pencil case?' said Jade.

168

The chalk dumped Lucy's pencil case in front of Baron de Couberpen. Baron de Couberpen beckoned to Stripes. She went over to the pencil case with a very puzzled look on her face.

Baron de Couberpen also beckoned to Penny, who walked over with an even more puzzled look on her face.

'I 'ave received some veree sad news. Some veree sad news indeed,' said Baron de Couberpen. 'Someone 'as been cheating!'

A gasp went around the stadium. Penny narrowed her eyes at Cheetah. But instead of looking guilty or worried, he looked quite smug and smarmy.

'Penny,' continued Baron de Couberpen.

'What?' said Penny, thinking Baron de Couberpen was blaming her.

'No, no, it is not you,' said Baron de Couberpen. 'I szust wanted you to repeat ze athletes' oath zat you took on be'alf of all ze athletes,' he continued, glaring at Stripes. 'Ze bit about ze rules.'

Penny recited: 'I promise to respect the rules of fair play and sportspencilship, without doping …'

'Could you say ze last two words again?' said Baron de Couberpen.

'Without doping …' repeated Penny.

'Wizout dopeeng!' yelled Baron de Couberpen. 'Zat means no banned substances. And what 'ave we got in 'ere?' he said, nodding to the piece of chalk closest to the zip of Lucy's pencil case.

The chalk pulled on the zip and a packaged cupcake fell out onto the sports field. All the spectators gasped. No one looked more shocked than Stripes.

'Zis cupcake does not comply with Standard 5.3.1.1 Subparagraph 2c of ze National 'Ealth Food Act!' yelled Baron de Couberpen, his face turning red with rage. 'It is a banned substance! You are disqualified!'

'But I …' began Stripes.

'Zip it!' said Baron de Couberpen.

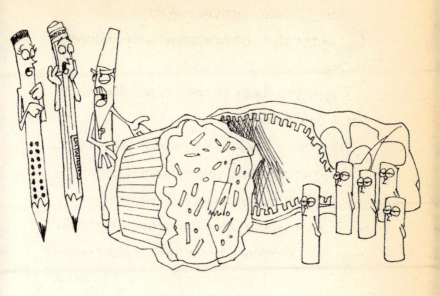

'But it's not mine …' Stripes protested.

'It was found in your penceel case,' said Baron de Couberpen.

Penny and Polly exchanged glances. They had both been inside Lucy's pencil case before, and there was barely room for all the pencils, let alone a cupcake!

'Take ze cupcake and ze athlete out of my sight,' said Baron de Couberpen to the chalk.

Stripes and the cupcake were escorted out of

the stadium, and the flag with the slice of cake on it was taken down from the flagpole.

'Let us continue,' said Baron de Couberpen.

Penny was so worried about what had happened to Stripes, that she hardly noticed what was happening in the competition. All the pencils took turns in jumping until it was only Penny and Cheetah left. Cheetah did a short jump, and it was Penny's turn. If she could jump further than Cheetah, she'd be the winner.

As Cheetah got up from the landing pad, he poked his tongue out at Penny. That was it. Her mind was made up.

Penny took all the bad thoughts of Cheetah out of her head, and imagined them in a spot just on the far side of the landing pad. Then she made up her mind to run and land foot first right in the middle of it.

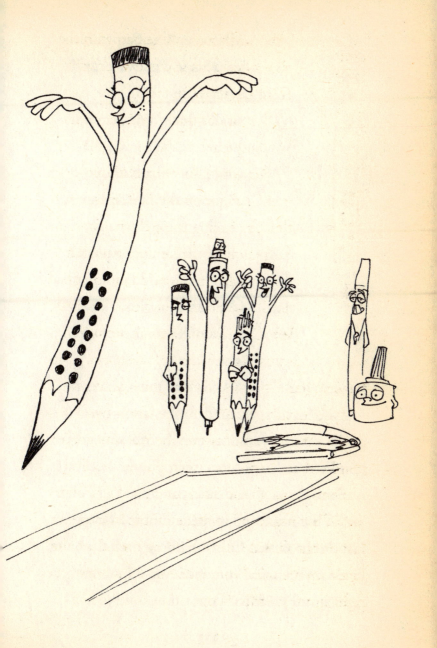

Baron de Couberpen blew his whistle. Penny started her run-up taking nice, easy strides that got faster and longer as she neared the jump line. She bounced right on the line and went sailing through the air, right over the landing pad and slap in the middle of her bad Cheetah thoughts.

Ralph's pencils went berserk.

'And the winner is, Penny!' shouted Amber from the commentary booth, so loudly that she barely needed a microphone. 'Second place goes to Cheetah and third place to Polly.'

'So the round-up at the end of the Long Jump section sees Cheetah ahead on five points, Ernie, Mack and Penny tied for second on three points, and Polly with one point,' said Jade.

'Which means, if you add Penny and Mack's scores together, Ralph's pencil case is winning!' said Amber.

'Shhh!' cautioned Jade. 'We're supposed to be impartial …'

'Join us tomorrow at the regatta centre in the bottom playground to see Penny and Mack blitz the field at rowing!' said Amber.

Chapter 14

Sabotage

The atmosphere in Ralph's pencil case was
nothing short of euphoric. The pencils were so
excited about their team mates doing well that
it was hard for Penny and Mack to even leave
the pencil case for classes.

177

When Ralph put his hand into the pencil case to pull Penny out for Maths Drawing, all the coloured pencils clung on to Penny so tightly that half of them came out with her!

'What's with you today?' Sarah asked Ralph as he spilled half the contents of his pencil case over the desk.

'My arm's been feeling funny ever since Bert knocked me over accidentally-on-purpose in Health class this morning,' said Ralph, rubbing his wrist.

'You really should have said something to Mrs Payne,' said Sarah, scowling at Bert.

Bert grabbed his drawing compass and pointed it at Sarah.

'Now turn around and be a good little teacher's pet,' said Bert.

'You *blunt* that thing at me again, and I really will tell,' said Sarah.

'The word is *point*, Monaghan. I thought you were supposed to be smart,' sneered Bert.

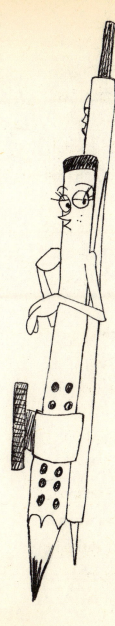

'And I thought points were supposed to be straight,' said Sarah, turning around and facing the front.

Penny peered over Ralph's shoulder and saw that the long, skinny leg of Bert's drawing compass was bent out of shape.

I wonder how that happened, thought Penny as Ralph screwed her into Mariko's hoop. Then she forgot all about it as she and Mariko span around and around drawing perfect circle after perfect circle.

Ralph's arm was still a little sore when he arrived at school the following morning.

'Your arm had better be ok soon,' warned Sarah. 'We only have two days of SHAM left, and

you're the only one who has a hope of beating
Bert. Remember how annoying he was when he
won the *Officer Cool* competition last year? Even
though he cheated …'

'I'd be well ahead of the big bully if my

scores didn't keep getting magically erased,' grumbled Ralph.

'I know,' said Sarah. 'And it wouldn't surprise me if Bert was behind this too!'

'Maybe we could change *his* score today …' suggested Ralph.

'There's no way we're going to stoop to his level,' said Sarah. 'If you're going to beat him, you're just going to have to do it fair and square.'

At the regatta centre that morning all the pencils were in high spirits. Ralph's pencils were happy that their pencil case was coming first overall. Sarah's pencils were happy that Polly had finally earned a point. Seán the Chewer's pencils were happy to be having a lesson away from the threat of Seán's teeth. And Bert's pencils were also happy, but in a kind of a nasty way.

'As rowing wasn't one of the qualification rounds, this is the first official race between the competitors,' said Jade over the loud speaker. 'How do you think they'll go?'

'Well, Sarah's pencil Polly has shown the best times in practice, but she'll also have stiff competition from Penny and Mack,' said Amber.

'And we shouldn't forget about Ernie and Cheetah. The favourite has crashed out a number of times in the Pencilympiad so far. It could be anybody's race,' said Jade.

'But it won't be yours,' muttered Cheetah at Polly out of the corner of his mouth.

'I beg your pardon?' said Polly.

'Attention!' called Baron de Couberpen to make sure all the competitors were ready.

Polly grabbed her oar and tried to forget about Cheetah.

'Go!' cried Baron de Couberpen.

'And they're off!' said Jade.

'Polly starts off nicely, getting to an early lead in Lane One. Penny in Lane Three is a close second, Mack and Cheetah not far behind. And Ernie appears to be going around in circles!' said Amber.

'Polly and Penny are opening up their lead. It seems to be a two-boat race,' said Jade.

Polly was rowing very hard when suddenly she noticed her foot was cold and wet. She looked down and noticed that there was a hole in the bottom of her boat and water was coming in. She was sinking!

'Oh, no,' said Polly, rowing even harder as her

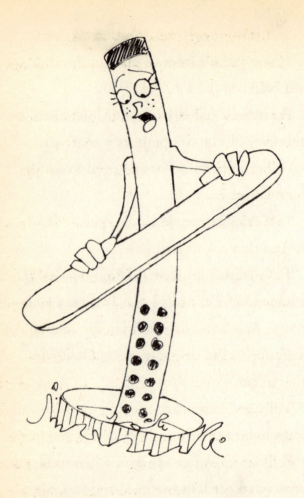

boat sank lower and lower in the water.

Two lanes away Penny rowed past her.

'Help!' cried Polly.

Penny looked over at her friend.

'What's wrong?' she asked.

'There's a hole in my boat, and I'm sinking!' said Polly.

Penny stopped racing and turned her boat around.

'What's she doing?' said Amber from the commentary booth.

'It looks like she's going to rescue Polly,' said Jade.

'But once she goes out of her lane she'll be disqualified!' said Amber. 'Don't do it you stupid …'

Amber's voice disappeared as Gloop un-plugged the speaker. He would have stern words with Amber later on.

Penny rowed over to Polly's lane, and just in time. Only the very top edge of Polly's boat was above water now. Penny rowed right alongside to what was left of the boat, and helped her friend to safety.

In the meantime, Cheetah, Mack and even Ernie crossed the finish line, but the biggest

cheer came when Penny rowed Polly across in fourth place.

After the race Penny waited with Polly while the pieces of chalk drained the trough and collected Polly's sunken boat.

'Here's your problem,' said the chalk-in-charge.

A hole had been drilled in the bottom of the boat, right in the middle of a big, black X.

Penny took one look at the X and shivered. She recognised the ink.

'Is that …?' began Polly.

'Black Texta ink,' nodded Penny. 'He's been here all along. And this time he's really got nasty.'

Back in Ralph's pencil case, Penny and Polly told Gloop, Mack and Smudge about their findings.

'And Cheetah's definitely in on it,' said Polly. 'He said something to me before the start of the race.'

'This is a truly evil side of Black Texta,' said Gloop. 'Messing with that boat was really dangerous. You could have drowned!'

Penny squeezed Polly's shoulder tightly.

'So we know he put the mark on the boat,' said Smudge. 'But who – or what – made the hole?'

'It would have to be something really sharp,' said Mack.

Penny went quiet. She'd seen something sharp recently. Something sharp that was a little bit broken, like it was used to do something it wasn't designed for.

'Bert's drawing compass!' said Penny. 'Bert pointed the compass at Sarah in class yesterday and the sharp end was all bent.'

'Well spotted, Penny,' said Gloop.

'But why did he attack my boat?' asked Polly. 'I thought Black Texta was Penny's enemy.'

'All this cheating seems to be aimed at the favourite for each round,' said Gloop. 'The three of you did best in the Sprint and there was glue in your lanes. Then Mack was best at high jump, and he was tripped up.'

'And Stripes was in the lead when that cupcake magically appeared in Lucy's pencil case,' said Penny.

'That's right,' said Mack. 'And Polly was the favourite today, so her boat was sabotaged.'

'And tomorrow's competition, the Archery, is the most dangerous of all,' said Gloop. 'Who's been doing the best in practice?'

Mack and Polly looked at Penny.

'That'd be me,' she said.

But the bottom of Polly's boat was not the only place black texta ink was found during the morning's Health class. Just as the children were sitting down at their desks again after doing their laps, Mrs Payne blew sharply on her whistle.

'WHO DID IT?' bellowed Mrs Payne.

The class looked silently from one to another.

'WELL?' yelled Mrs Payne.

Bravely, Sarah put up her hand.

'Did what, Mrs Payne?' asked Sarah.

'SCRIBBLED OUT ALL THE SCORES!'
growled Mrs Payne, holding the SHAMPERS
score sheet up.

There was black texta ink all over the score sheet.

'There is no way we can use these scores now,' shouted Mrs Payne, a little more quietly. 'But never mind. We shall have a proper final tomorrow. A race, combining all the skills you have learned: speed, strength and tidiness!'

Chapter 15

Penny on Target

Penny awoke on the last day of the Pencilympiad even more nervous than she had been on
the first day. Bert's pencils working together
to make Cheetah win the competition was
one thing, but knowing Black Texta was out
there was something else entirely – especially

when he was after Penny in Archery, the most dangerous event of the Pencilympiad.

Penny's friends tried to console her. Gloop and Smudge promised to be on the lookout for Black Texta in the stands, and even Little Mack said he would keep a special eye out when Mack was busy in the competition. They decided not to alert the rest of the pencils to the danger, as they didn't want to cause panic.

As usual, Jade and Amber were already commentating when Penny nervously walked into the stadium.

'... with only one event to go, Cheetah is in an unbeatable position on eight points,' Jade was saying.

'Being three points ahead of the nearest competitor, even if Cheetah gets no points for this event, the worst he can do is tie for first in the individual championship,' agreed Amber.

'But Cheetah still needs to finish well ahead of Mack and Penny for Bert's pencil case to win the overall championship,' said Jade.

'With Penny on three points and Mack on five, together they have eight points, making Ralph's pencil case tied with Bert's, so it's not all over yet folks,' said Amber.

'It will also be a tough battle for third with Ernie on four points, and Polly bringing up the rear on one point,' said Jade.

'Of course, it all could have been a different story if Penny hadn't relinquished her lead in the rowing yesterday to save Polly,' said Amber.

'Hopefully we won't see the need for such heroics today,' said Jade.

Fat chance of that, thought Penny gloomily, scanning the stands for any sign of Black Texta.

The Archery stadium was shaped like a horse shoe, with the open end along the wall where the notice board was. A row of five, round targets had been pinned up, one for each of the competitors. The centre of each target was yellow, surrounded by rings of red, blue, black and white. Opposite the targets, at the far end of the stadium were five rulers and rubber bands.

To make the event as exciting as possible, Baron de Couberpen decided to make the pencils fire in reverse points order again, but this time with a twist. Polly was to go first, followed by Ernie, Mack and Cheetah, then Penny, because she was the best at Archery and her shot would decide the pencil case championship.

Penny watched nervously as Polly loaded herself into the bow. All Sarah's pencils were chanting 'Pol-ly! Pol-ly!' Polly stretched her body out, took careful aim, and fired. She flew towards the notice board, straight as an arrow, and landed on the yellow circle.

'And Polly scores ten points!' said Amber.

Next up was Ernie. Seán the Chewer's pencils whistled and cheered as the little pencil climbed into his bow. He was very nervous, and wobbled around quite a bit before steadying himself. Ernie let go of the ruler, and shot

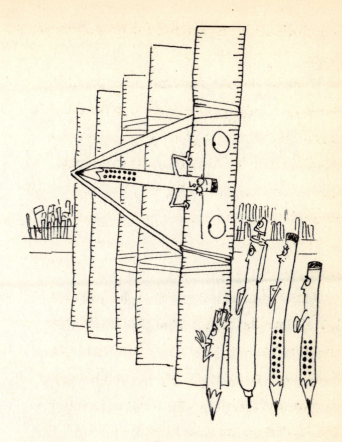

towards the notice board, landing left of centre on the yellow band of the target.

'That's nine points for Ernie,' said Jade.

'And now it's Mack's turn!' said Amber, clapping and swinging a noisemaker into the microphone.

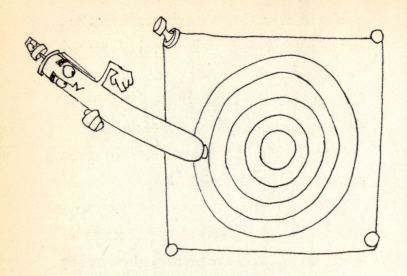

Mack grabbed hold of the ruler and eased the rubber back with his toe. He was taking even longer to find his target than Ernie. Penny looked at Mack closely and noticed he was squinting. Something shiny was reflecting in his eyes. Mack steadied himself and fired. The shot was wide, and he only just struck the white outer circle of his target, getting one point.

'And that's a terrible shot from Mack,' said Jade from the commentary booth.

'Let's see if Cheetah can do any better,' said Amber.

Cheetah confidently strode over to his bow and climbed aboard. All Bert's pencils started making a deep *whoop, whoop, whooping* sound. Cheetah took aim and fired. He sailed through the air, landing on the red ring of the target.

'And Cheetah hits the red ring, scoring seven points,' said Jade gloomily.

'Let's hope Penny can do better,' said Amber. 'She needs to get a six for Ralph's pencil case to tie with Bert's or a seven to be the outright winner.'

'Of course, if she misses, Bert's pencil case will win,' said Jade.

'It's all down to this shot,' Amber said as Penny clambered into the bow.

'The pressure's on,' said Jade, as Penny stretched her leg out, feeling the weight

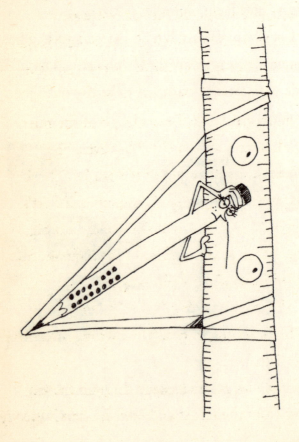

of the rubber band anxious to propel her forward.

Penny took careful aim at the centre of her target. But for some reason, she was finding it hard to see. Something bright was shining in her eyes. Penny remembered seeing Mack squint, and suddenly she knew it wasn't coincidence. Someone had sabotaged Mack's turn by shining a mirror in his eyes, and they were trying to do the same to her!

With great care, Penny let go of the ruler with one arm and shielded her eyes. She looked in the direction of the bright light. It was coming from directly underneath Bert's flagpole. Penny thought she could see a big, black shape at the bottom of the flagpole. She angled her body around to face it.

'What is she doing?' said Amber.

'She's aiming in totally the wrong direction!' said Jade.

Penny let go. She soared through the air, away from the target and into the stand directly

below Bert's flagpole. Instead of going through paper into the corkboard, Penny's lead pierced through a black plastic texta lid.

'It looks like she's hit ...' said Amber.

'Is that really … Black Texta?' said Jade.

Black Texta's lid was pinned to the flagpole by Penny's foot. They both glared at each other.

'Look's like you lost,' said Black Texta defiantly.

'I'm not the only loser today,' said Penny.

Gloop, Smudge and Baron de Couberpen raced to the top of the stands. Amber appeared with her portable microphone.

'What is thees?' exclaimed Baron de Couberpen, his voice echoing around the stadium as the sound went from Amber's microphone through the loud speakers.

'This is Black Texta,' said Penny. 'He's been helping Cheetah win by sabotaging all the events.'

A gasp went around the stadium.

'See that mirror in his hands?' continued Penny. 'He was shining it in Mack's face, and then my face so that we'd miss our targets today. And yesterday, he forced Bert's drawing compass to make a hole in Polly's boat.'

'And the day before that he planted the cupcake in Lucy's pencil case, and the day before that he tripped Mack up in the High Jump,' said Smudge.

'Not to mention the glue in Penny, Mack and Polly's lanes in the Sprint,' said Gloop.

Baron de Couberpen looked at the gathered crowd of pencils.

'Why was none of zees reported to me?' he demanded.

'Because when I tried to tell you about Cheetah cheating in the qualification, you weren't interested,' said Penny.

Baron de Couberpen turned very red. Penny thought he was going to get very angry with her. But instead, he was angry with himself.

'It seems I 'ave put my own dreams of eternal sporteeng gloree a'ead of ze most important sporting value, fair play,' said Baron de Couberpen. 'I am veree sorree to 'ave put you all in such danger.'

He turned to Gloop.

'My fat friend, I leave you in charge of adding up ze final scores and 'anding out ze medals. In ze meantime, I 'ave an appropriate punishment for zeese two cheaters. Chalk, grab Cheetah and zis strange-looking implement and come with me.'

'Where are you taking us?' Black Texta asked as the chalk grabbed him and Cheetah.

'To boot camp,' said Baron de Couberpen. 'But not szust anee boot camp. A special *French* boot camp.'

And without a further word – French or otherwise – Baron de Couberpen and the chalk marched Black Texta and Cheetah out of the classroom.

'Well,' said Gloop, taking the microphone from Amber. 'That brings us to our medal ceremony. Would the athletes please gather in front of the podium in five minutes while I do some quick adding up.'

Things were just as exciting out in the play-ground. Mrs Payne had marked out a running course with traffic cones. But it wasn't any ordinary running course. Instead of being a flat, basically oval track, it went into the adventure playground, over the play equipment and around corners. And that wasn't all. Every so often there were heavy-looking barbells or other pieces of sporting equipment with numbers on a big sign next to them.

'This is an obstacle course,' bellowed Mrs Payne. 'You have to run around it as fast as you can, including all the obstacles. Some of the obstacles you have to climb over, others are an activity you must do, like doing ten push-ups, twenty skips with a skipping rope, or lifting weights. It's all explained on the sign next to the obstacle.

'The person who finishes the obstacle course in the shortest time, completing ALL the obstacles, will be declared class champion. And be warned, there will be severe penalties if you skip an obstacle.

'Are you ready? On your marks, get set, go!'

Mrs Payne blew her whistle and the race began. The children sprinted along the narrow path between the traffic cones. As they reached the first corner, Ralph, Bert, and surprisingly Sarah were in the lead.

After rounding the corner, they came to
the first obstacle – the A-frame fort in the
adventure playground. Ralph jumped towards
the fort, landing on the third step and quickly

208

climbed his way up. Bert was a step or two behind him, and pulled at Ralph's foot, but Ralph managed to kick away and kept going. He made it over the top and was going down the other side when Bert had a second, nasty idea. Bert purposefully let Ralph get ahead so that Bert's feet would be where Ralph's fingers were as he climbed down the ladder on the other side. Bert stamped hard on Ralph's fingers, and Ralph lost his grip, falling the four feet to the ground.

Luckily Ralph didn't hurt himself when he landed, and despite his sore fingers was able to keep going.

The next obstacle was the barbells. The sign said '10' so Ralph lifted the barbells up ten times. When he got to his eighth lift, Bert had already finished and was running ahead.

'I think he's cheating!' panted Ralph to Sarah.

'Don't worry about it,' said Sarah, her face bright red from the weight of the barbells. 'You can run faster than him, now go beat him fair and square!'

Ralph did his final two lifts, dropped the barbells – 'Ow!' said Sarah as they accidentally landed on her toe – and sprinted after Bert to the next obstacle, the skipping ropes. The task here was to do twenty skips in a row without getting your feet caught up in the rope, and Mrs Payne was watching very carefully. Ralph started skipping, remembering what Sarah had said, and finished his twenty skips before Bert, who kept getting his feet caught up in the rope.

Ralph took off and headed for the next obstacle. This time it was the monkey bars. The task was to make it across without falling. If anyone fell off, they had to go back to the start. Mrs Sword was on hand at this obstacle, watching out for cheats.

Ralph made it across the monkey bars in the first go, and ran along to the next obstacle, push-ups.

He had just finished his ten when Sarah and Bert arrived, neck and neck.

'Go Ralph!' called Sarah as Ralph stood up and ran towards the last obstacle. This was a basketball hoop, and Ralph had to shoot twenty baskets before getting to the finish line.

Ralph shot the first ten easily, *whoosh! whoosh! whoosh!* then Bert arrived. He said all sorts of mean things to Ralph, but Ralph concentrated and didn't let himself get distracted. Then Bert tried something sneakier. The next time Ralph's ball headed for the hoop, Bert threw his own ball at it, knocking both balls off target.

'What are you doing?' yelled Ralph.

'Stopping you winning,' said Bert nastily.

'Why don't you just try to win fairly?' asked Ralph.

'I don't care about winning,' said Bert. 'As long as you lose.'

Whoosh! A third ball went through the hoop perfectly.

Whoosh!

Bert and Ralph turned to see Sarah throwing the basketball.

Whoosh!

'You don't even care if you get beaten by a *girl*?' said Sarah to Bert.

Whoosh!

It did the trick. Instead of deliberately throwing his ball at Ralph's Bert started aiming for the hoop. But he was too slow. Ralph was already ten points ahead, and before Bert had even scored five, Ralph was on his way to the finish line, followed closely by Sarah.

Sarah and Ralph shook hands as Mrs Payne wrote their times down on their score sheets.

'Let's go and wash that hand Bert stepped on, just to make sure he didn't do any real damage!' said Sarah.

Chapter 16

The Medal Ceremony

Penny, Polly, Mack and Ernie gathered in front of the podium to wait for Gloop and the results.

Gloop waddled onto the field, to loud applause from everyone.

'We are missing an athlete,' said Gloop. 'Would Stripes step forward please.'

All Lucy's pencils cheered and clapped as they pushed Stripes out from the stand to where the other pencils were standing.

'Thank you all for participating so well in this Pencilympiad,' said Gloop.

All the pencils in the audience clapped.

'And thank you also to the crowd,' continued Gloop. 'Your support and enthusiasm has made this Pencilympiad such a memorable occasion.'

The athletes put their hands above their heads and gave the crowd a huge applause.

'Now to the results,' said Gloop. 'The winner of the individual event, on six points, is Ernie!'

All Seán the Chewer's pencils jumped up and down and hugged each other as Ernie stepped onto the podium to receive his gold medal.

'In second place, with five points, is Mack!' said Gloop.

Ralph's pencils clapped and threw roses as Mack climbed onto the podium to receive the silver medal.

'And in equal third place, on four points, are Polly and Stripes!'

Polly and Stripes held hands and stepped up onto the podium together, leaving Penny alone in front of the podium. Sarah and Lucy's pencils all cheered together.

'And now,' said Gloop, 'to the most special award of all.'

A hush went around the stadium. 'Rather than giving the team award to the pencil case with the most points, I have decided to give this award to the pencil who showed the greatest team spirit of all the pencils in the Pencilympiad.'

The pencils in the crowd all whispered approvingly.

'You often hear teachers and parents say it is not whether you win or lose, it's how you play the game,' continued Gloop. 'Well, in this Pencilympiad we have seen a fine example of that. One pencil in particular showed utmost bravery and sportspencillike behaviour several times throughout the competition. She saved a pencil from drowning, and today, she sacrificed a win in the interests of fair play. This year's best and fairest award goes to Penny!'

The whole stadium burst into applause as Penny stepped forward to receive her medal. Ernie then put a hand out to Penny to help her step onto the gold medal platform.

The pencils were cheering so loudly, that they only heard the children's footsteps coming back to the classroom in the nick of time.

'Quick! Back to your pencil cases!' said Gloop.

The writing implements all hurried back to the children's pencil cases and the remaining pieces of chalk cleared away the archery stadium.

The children entered the classroom and sat down at their desks.

Mrs Payne blew her whistle.

'Ralph was the fastest across the finish line today, but it's now time to work out who the real winner is,' she boomed. 'Who can tell me the three principles of good health?'

Sarah put up her hand.

'Yes, Sarah?' yelled Mrs Payne.

'Speed, strength and tidiness,' said Sarah.

'Exactly. We know who was fastest and strongest from the race, but who is the tidiest?' shouted Mrs Payne, walking around the children's desks. 'Put your hands on the desk, palms up!'

Mrs Payne inspected the children's hands. Ralph's and Sarah's were sparkling clean, having just washed them after the race.

'Very good, very good,' murmured
Mrs Payne as she walked past Ralph and Sarah.
When she got to the row behind them, she
boomed, 'A-ha! WHAT IS THAT ON YOUR
HANDS?'

Bert blushed bright red, and tried to sit on
his hands, but Mrs Payne had him firmly by the
wrists.

'Is that black texta ink?' she cried.

'Y-yes,' admitted Bert.

'The same black texta ink that has been
scribbled all over the score sheet? Well, is it?'
Mrs Payne demanded.

Ralph and Sarah turned around, smiling.

'It was a mistake ...' began Bert.

'Oh, there's been no mistake,' yelled
Mrs Payne. 'And a whole month's worth of
detention for you!'

All the children in the class put their hands
over their mouths and giggled.

'Now, since the rest of you have performed
so well all month, and have clean hands,'

continued Mrs Payne, 'I let Mrs Sword bring in a treat.'

Mrs Sword walked into the classroom carrying a cake. But not just any cake, a chocolate cream sponge made with real chocolate and butter and sugar.

The children all ate their slices greedily, not leaving a single crumb behind.

'Well, I might not have taught them good eating habits, but at least I have taught them to be tidy,' said Mrs Payne to Mrs Sword.

'Mrs Payne will be leaving now, class. What do you say?' said Mrs Sword.

'Goodbye, Mrs Payne,' chorused the children.

'Goodbye, class,' yelled Mrs Payne.

'She wasn't so bad in the end,' Sarah whispered to Ralph.

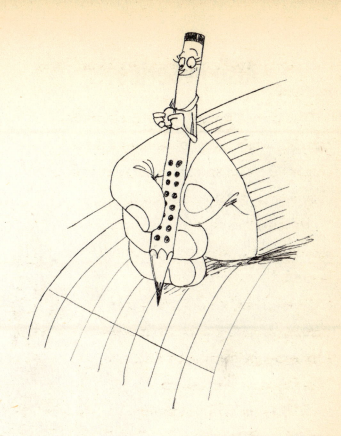

'I thought she was a real pain in the –' began
Bert.

'Bert! If you say another word, that will be
two months worth of detention for you!' said
Mrs Sword.

'It's good to have things back to normal,'
thought Ralph, pulling Penny out to write with.

Penny couldn't have agreed more.

Also in Series...

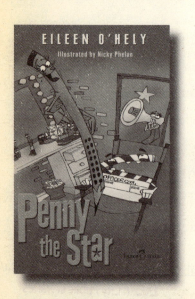